Home is a Fire
a novel

JORDAN NASSER

To all the people I shouldn't have kissed.

1

THE SUBWAY

The 4 train is barreling down Lexington Avenue and I can see the reflection of my face in the glass of the subway door. I'm not pretty. My mind is wandering to when I first moved to New York from Tennessee, twelve years ago. I was twenty-one, fresh out of college, and ready to take on the world. In my first week in the city, I vividly remember squeezing myself onto a packed subway car similar to this one, with a sweat inducing lack of air conditioning. There were a million hands, arms and bags stretching between poles, doors and ceiling, like a Twister board on the move, yet no one was touching anybody else. New Yorkers have this uncanny ability to live in this huge metropolis of millions, and yet never violate the space of a stranger. It's an unwritten rule.

I had sardined myself next to a lady in a dark blue polyester suit jacket, skirt and running shoes. Very *Working Girl*. She was staring off into the train doors with a glazed look that was a mixture of boredom and acceptance, the reflection of her face next to mine. I was all smiles and newbie excitement. Slowly, dully and with no emotion, her lips parted. "I been riding this train for fifteen years," she said to no one in particular, her eyes never moving. I glanced away from her reflection, creased my brow and assured myself that I would never become her.

And now, here I am twelve years later staring at my own reflection, the corners of my lips resting softly somewhere down near my toes. My boyfriend, David, is talking non-stop about our upcoming wedding. We are on a packed express train on our way to City Hall to apply for our Marriage License, and he's ticking off the items on our to-do list. His lips are moving and his hands are fluttering about excitedly, like a kid who just had too many Pixy Stix. I'm leaning on the back of a seat, between the pole and the door with my hands stuffed in the pockets of my jeans and he's practically dancing on the tips of his toes in front of me, "surfing" hands-free. He refuses to touch any surface on the train. Ever.

"And then we have to look at that spot in Central Park again, remember?" he started. "Not the one where Tony and Jill got married. That was awful. All those screaming kids, right? I mean, how could they? That's why I don't trust wedding planners. Didn't they check that space at all beforehand? And I know you don't want a religious ceremony, but do you really trust that online preacher license thing? Can you really get ordained online? I mean, yeah, it would be great for Marcos to marry us, but is it legal? Really? Because I don't wanna run into problems with our taxes later, you know? God knows we don't wanna get audited. But we can talk about that later. I mean, there's so much more we have to decide." He paused for effect. "I think I really wanna wear white. Can I wear white? Is that crazy? I mean, I know we're not virgins and all, but do you really think that matters these days? Besides, hello, we're gay! All rules out the window, right? HA! My mother is freaking. I mean, she's way too excited about this already, but she is gonna get worse. Total control. She'll want total control over this thing. But I promise you, babe, I'm not letting her anywhere near it. It's just you and me against the world! It's gonna KILL me, but I'm gonna pull this off all by myself. Just you wait! OH! And…"

And I'm staring at his face and I can hear what he's saying, but I don't think I can listen anymore. My heart is racing and all I can feel is the *bump, bump, whack* of the tracks below my feet as the snippets of graffiti on the tunnel walls race by. The beads of perspiration start to trickle down my forehead. My stomach is rising up to meet my throat, I can feel my back get prickly with sweat and I'm about to ruin another shirt. The train pulls to a stop at 14th Street and I instinctively shift to one side of the door as the city begins to move all around me. David is still talking. It's as if he has taken control over all of the oxygen in the subway car, and I'm on life support. "Next stop, Brooklyn Bridge/City Hall," the pre-recorded voice speaks out, jarring me back to reality.

The doors chime to warn they are closing and I step off the train, backwards, as they shut in front of me. David, in a panic, rushes forward with his hands pressed to the glass door. "Oh, my god! Oh, my god! What happened?!" he screams through the glass. "It's the next stop! Oh, my god! Don't panic. It's OK! Get the next train and I'll wait for you!"

"I'm breaking up with you," I say, almost to myself.

"Wait?! What?! I can't, I... I can't hear you."

"I'M BREAKING UP WITH YOU," I scream, and repeat. "I'm breaking up with you. I'm sorry."

The car is pulling away and suddenly David is no longer speaking. His hands are still pressed to the glass. His face is white and pale and frightened and... gone, to Brooklyn Bridge/City Hall, without me.

I take another step back and feel faint. I can't breathe. I need air. The thick heat of the tunnel is pressing down on me as I bound up the steps two by two to Union Square Park and grab the nearest free bench. There's a homeless man to my left with his entire world of belongings strapped to a wire shopping cart, like a Grand Canyon mule made of blue plastic and metal and string. He is the "King of the Magpies," and he collects every shiny object in his path. To my right, a tourist is eating an overpriced street pretzel.

I pull my phone from my pocket and stare at it numbly, knowing there is only one call I can make. There's only one person who can make me feel better right now.

The phone rings, and I get her voicemail. "Hey Mom, it's me, Derek. I'm coming home."

■ ■ ■

The next few weeks are a blur of activity. Breaking up with David is one thing, but breaking up with New York is an entirely new level of heartache. New York is like the coolest girl in school, and you just want to be her friend. Now I'm ditching her for someone else, somewhere else, and she's not happy. Neither am I. The next few weeks are spent crying, partying and packing, in that order. Oh, and I have to quit my job.

I work part-time as an instructor at a theatre workshop space that caters to privileged kids from Long Island and wannabe actresses from Iowa with big dreams and fat wallets. I work mainly with the kids, leading classes in improvisational techniques and basic monologues. It's less about Shakespeare and more about Shake 'n Bake commercials. We call it "schmacting." There are lots of jazz hands and mimed glass walls. The rest of my time is devoted to auditioning. I've booked a few voiceovers and the occasional corporate video, but in twelve years of working my ass off, my big break hasn't arrived. The closest I ever came to fame was a walk-on in a rap music video. I wasn't supposed to have any lines, but at the last minute I improvised a character out of thin air. The director loved it, but the "artist" hated it. I could tell by the subtle way he kept kicking his boot into the door of the rented Mercedes SL on set. Needless to say, my brilliance ended up on the cutting room floor.

At first I try to sell as much as I can, and then I realize that New York is a city of givers and takers. I'm supposed to give and someone else is supposed to take everything I own off my hands, for free. I end up listing all my furniture on Craigslist as a "Come and Get it!" I don't make a dime. In a way, it's freeing and terrifying all at once. I question myself constantly. What am I doing? I had everything. Well, kind of. Work was actually fun,

I had a career goal, great friends, and a man who loved me, until I literally stepped out of his life.

We still haven't spoken. I mean, I can't. He's tried and I just can't. What am I supposed to say? "Sorry I said I would marry you and I told you I loved you, and I really probably do, but there was just this voice in my head that said *run now* or forever hold your peace?" I know it seems cold and heartless, but I tell myself that nothing I can say to him will make it any better, so it's better to say nothing at all. It's a lie, but it makes me feel better. Will it make him feel any better? Probably not. Part of me just wants him to hate me so I won't have to deal with the mess I created. I have this terrible habit of running away, and here I go again.

I've booked my flight to Tennessee. I've only spoken to Mom once since my freak out on the subway. She called to ask me why I left her a voicemail, when I should know that "nobody leaves voicemails anymore. Why didn't you write me on Facebook? And besides, you know I can't remember the damn password for my cell phone messages. I had to get the guy at the store to help me again." Already I'm having second thoughts about this being the right move for me. But I know I need to go somewhere, so it may as well be back home. I just need a stress-free existence for a while. I need to figure out my life and just relax, while eating my mom's chicken fried steak and homemade biscuits. I can hang out with my friends from high school and I can start jogging regularly, again! I used to jog three times a week, but for some reason I just stopped when David and I got together. I'm not fat at all, considering the amount of vodka I have consumed in the years I've lived here, but the fact that

I could never really afford a huge trip to the grocery store has helped to keep my weight down. That and the pace of life in New York City.

I take the six boxes that contain what's left of my life and head down the elevator. Thankfully, there is a shipping center just across the street. There's a lot of door propping with feet and boxes and I'm sweating like crazy by the time I get everything over there. I am only now realizing that most of my friends in New York, with the exception of David, are mainly acquaintances, and the rest are just so extremely busy that they don't even have time to give me a proper send off. Thanks, guys. I tried to call Marcos, but he didn't answer. I'm pretty sure David got custody of him in the divorce. A million forms and too many dollars later, the boxed remnants of my life are heading down to Tennessee, via the Memphis sorting hub.

I walk back into my building and climb out the window. Over and up the fire escape and I am face to face with the Chrysler Building. The taxis are honking below and I can see the sun setting over the West Side. Good-bye, New York. It's been fun.

2

THE DUST EXPERIMENT

I'm just finally, really getting comfortable in my extremely narrow 22" seat when the flight attendant announces that we need to shut off our electronic devices, as we are making our initial descent into the wilds of Tennessee. The air feels cold and humid at the same time, if that's even possible. I'm afraid and excited and exhausted and terrified all at once, but I'm beginning to accept the fact that I made a choice. Was it the right one?

I slip my magazine back into my trendy canvas tote bag and place it at my feet. The window is cold as I lean my forehead against it and peer down to the landscape below. I can't help but think it looks gorgeous. There are trees everywhere, not just confined to parks and popping up out of the concrete on the occasional Park Avenue corner! I always felt so sorry for those scrappy city trees with the little metal signs stating "Please curb your dog" chained to their trunks. Yeah, right. In

Tennessee, we let our trees (and dogs) roam free, as long as they vote Republican.

The plane lands quite smoothly and we begin to head towards the gate. The flight attendant reminds us to keep our mobile phones powered down until the captain turns off the fasten seat belts light. I immediately turn mine on and start looking for a signal. If they get upset with me I'll just pretend I don't speak English. It rarely worked in a city as diverse as New York, but here I could easily get away with it.

I grab my coat and leather duffel from the overhead bin, shifting my feet along in the chain gang towards the door. "Buh bye! Bye! Bye bye! Good-bye!" and then, "See you soon!" No you won't. I made the choice to leave you. Now I'm stuck here. Is it too late to turn this plane around?

The terminal is warm, almost welcoming. It feels different from New York. It smells like bacon and maple syrup. My panic begins to subside as I walk through the familiar hall, filled with healthy food choices like Burger Shak, Wok/Don't Wok and Ricky's Super Subs. Do I have time for one of those cinnamon pretzels? Damn! How does my mind shift to craving sugar so quickly? I've barely landed. Note to self: remember that you like green salads, dressing on the side and hold the bacon and fried chicken nuggets.

I exit the security area and head towards baggage claim. My mom, Audrey, is there waiting for me. She's slumped on the pleather bench, legs crossed, one shoe dangling and dancing from her foot, arms in her lap.

She looks up at me, smiles and cocks her head. "Hi, sweetie! You look thin."

"And you look tired," I say. "And I've always been thin. You know that. C'mere."

I reach down to pull her up in my arms. I tower above her, my chin resting on top of her head. She's warm and soft and smells like fried food and her familiar perfume and it all feels just right.

"Let's get your bag, sweetie. Your uncle Barry's excited to see you. He has a Bears' Club meeting right now, but he'll be back later, when you're settled."

And that's that. Easy, right?

■ ■ ■

The house is exactly as I remembered it, only a little worse for wear. It's not actually the house I grew up in. After my parents split when I was a kid, my mom moved us to a smaller home. I hated it at first. It's located back towards the woods, off the beaten path, and my adolescent mind associated that with poor, poor and poor. Now I know better. She did the best she could with the resources she had, and I've really grown to love the place.

Over the years the small A-frame house has grown a bit with rambling additions and add-ons. It's not perfect, but it's as close to home as I've got right now.

"Holy shit, Mother. What the hell happened?" I dropped my bags on the floor, near the wood-burning stove.

"Oh, honey, you know I get so excited when you come home! Now... GO!"

She's staring at me excitedly, as if I am a contestant in a game show and I have just been given ninety seconds to complete the task at hand to win an amazing six day/seven night trip to Puerto Vallarta, Mexico.

But in reality, she is putting me to work.

Before me, on the dining room table, lie the entire contents of her home. And by *entire contents*, I mean every knick-knack, vase, candlestick, dusty flower arrangement, antique bottle and rusted cookie tin within a fifty mile radius. Mom is a collector. Of everything. And she expects me to re-stage her house. Right now.

I look at her with *I will kill you this very instant* eyes, but secretly I love it. With as much faux reluctance as I can muster, I dive towards the table and start the task of reconstructing the magic, staging her collection of dusty treasures around the room on tables and bookshelves, turning our little A-frame into a show home once more. She sits on the couch *ooh-ing* and *ah-ing*. "Oh, sweetie, that looks great! You're so much better at this than I am," she said.

"It would look better if you dusted once in a blue moon, Mom. You could start a few biology experiments in this place." I held up my fingers, covered in a greyish brown fuzz.

"Oh, I am! I'm trying to see how high dust can get before it falls over," she said, with a seriously wicked grin. That's my mom. I missed her.

I stand back and take a look at my handiwork. It was fun, but there's no way I'm doing this in every room tonight. It's not a very big house, actually. Mom's bedroom is downstairs off the kitchen. My old room is upstairs, across from the guest room, which is now my uncle Barry's room. Barry is Mom's brother, and he only moved in recently, after the death of his wife, my aunt Janey. They were married just over forty years, and when

Janey passed away from breast cancer, Mom invited Barry to move in with her. I guess they both figured it wouldn't hurt having that extra bit of support. They keep each other company, as they each go about their own lives.

"Barry will just love this when he sees it. You've done such a nice job, sweetie."

"How's he doing?" I asked. I knew he had had a tough time after Janey's passing.

"Well, you know," she said, furrowing her brow. "We all do the best we can. It's nice having him around. I have someone to cook for and he has someone to yell at. Just like old times!"

I carried my bags upstairs and set them down in the hallway. Out of curiosity, I pushed open the door to Uncle Barry's room. Formerly known as the Guest Room, but really the Junk Room, this part of the house used to be uninhabitable. Mom had it stocked to the ceiling with old clothes, quilt pieces, Christmas ornaments, sewing paraphernalia and a few hundred outdated appliances.

"Wow. He's done a nice job," I said. "It's totally different."

"Yep. All cleaned up," she said with a smile. "Barry's friends at The Bears' Club put up a nice shed for me out in the back. All my things are there when I need them. You know, I'm going to start that quilt soon."

Mom has been "going to start that quilt" since I was ten. "Uh huh," I muttered, as I slid open the closet doors.

"Um… Mom? Why are there women's clothes in here?"

"Well, you know Barry. He loves his personal treasures just as much as I do. He says he just couldn't part with Janey's things."

I've had enough reminiscing, and the emotions are catching up with me. "Love ya, Mom, but I'm exhausted. I'm heading off to bed. Long trip."

I give her a kiss on the cheek and cross the hall to open the door to my room. Immediately I'm a teenager again. My comic books are still on the shelves, my *Interview* magazines stacked on the floor by the bed. There's a giant blue Swatch watch wall clock, second hand silently ticking away, as if the 80s never ended.

I sit quietly on my bed, staring at my Madonna *Truth or Dare* poster. This is all happening so fast. Leaving David, New York, my life. I'm in Tennessee?

Fuck, I need a drink.

3

THE FIRELIGHT

When I first started driving in Parkville at sixteen years old there were two red lights running the entire stretch of our main drag, Commodore Avenue. Now my frustration is mounting as the car is crawling along, catching every single light, past every chain restaurant known to man. When did my small town become the epicenter of gluttony?

Thank God that The Firelight still exists. The Firelight has stood on this hallowed site for generations, and lives today to continue to serve the hordes of college football-loving students and returning graduates (and plenty of non-graduates) with an endless stream of beer on tap, pool tables for hire, and the best damn jukebox in the state. Where else on Earth can you queue up Patsy Cline's "Walking After Midnight," followed by "Head Like a Hole" by Nine Inch Nails? And don't even get me started on the graffiti in the bathrooms: epic masterpieces in industrial black magic markers, with more of an emphasis on snark, rather than smut.

I look back eagerly towards our favorite booth, and there are my friends Bammy, Kit and Tommy, waiting for me, surrounded by pitchers of beer. I can barely hold back the enormous grin as it spreads across my face and I have to consciously stop myself from letting out a girl scream.

Rebecca "Bammy" Talbot was proudly raised by her Daughters of the Confederacy mother in Alabama, but moved to Tennessee when she was fourteen. We have been inseparable ever since. As freshman at our local state college, we were well under the legal drinking age, but Bammy figured out a way around that. She was a genius at subterfuge. With a surgeon's precision, she would take a ripe watermelon, cut it into chunks, cover it all in vodka, and then place the bite sized vodka-soaked morsels in plastic sandwich bags. As eighteen year olds, the doorman would let us into The Firelight, but we weren't allowed to drink. This was noted by a big black X drawn on the backs of our hands with a magic marker. "Yes, sir!" she'd say with a smile, as we headed towards a wagon wheel table, plastic bags magically appearing from her oversized purse. If anyone ever needed an excuse, a reason or an escape route, we asked Bammy. I have always said that if Harper Lee had ever met our girl, I'd venture to say she would have many more stories to tell.

Bammy's mother had insisted that her daughter pursue a "proper" education, so that when the approved suitor called on her, she would be well versed in the Liberal Arts. The French language was a must, and surprisingly, Bammy excelled. She said it had to something to do with her love of wine. She dated her fair share of Chips and Teddys and Parkers, but her mother's efforts towards creating the perfect debutante fell flat. Bammy was just too smart for all of them. After a semester abroad in Paris, Bammy decided to become a self-supporting French teacher, rather than the woman behind the man. She taught at our local high school for a few years, but had recently been offered the job as Vice Principal, insuring that no man we graduated with would ever want her.

Kit Lange and I met in college, and she was my everything. My twin, my mirrored other self, she understood me like no one else ever could or would. In college, Kit wrote stories about me set in New York, Paris and London and slipped them into my textbooks and coat pockets. She always dreamed bigger for me than I could ever imagine for myself. She had been unlucky in love, but she was now steadily dating a great guy named Shawn, a local guitar hero who played bass in a funky cover band called Shock the Monkey. A girl we went to school with recently asked her "Did your parents freak out that you're dating a black guy?" She responded by saying "Did your parents freak out that you're a moron?" And that was the end of that conversation.

I'd known Tommy Pruitt the longest. Memories of middle school Field Days and burlap sack races blended seamlessly into stories of drunken all-nighters and "remember whens." Tommy was the best straight friend a gay guy could ever have. Period.

"HEY! Derek!" Screams and squeals and hugs and kisses. I love New York. I really, really do. But there is truly something special about coming home to the people who have honestly known you since before you knew yourself.

"Tell us everything!" Bammy is taking charge, as usual. "Did you really leave David?! Are you here for good? And why on *Earth* would you come back here?! Are you here to rescue us? Oh, my god! We need more drinks!"

Kit is holding a Cruella de Vil cigarette holder, even though smoking is not allowed in the bar. She doesn't care. The cigarette is unlit; it's all for looks, and she's pulling it off, as usual. Her bowling bag purse is parked by her side.

"Baby," said Kit, reaching out and touching my arm, "it's so great to see you! *We. Love. You.* We can't wait to hear everything. Tell us the story!"

Tommy is just leaning back with a cold beer in his hand. He has a sweet, happy grin on his face, watching the craziness unfold.

"What can I say?" I smiled. "I was craving a good biscuit."

■ ■ ■

"I know I gave up beer for my diet, but this whiskey is killing me, y'all!"

Bammy is reaching for her third Jack and Diet Coke, and the rest of us are in Rolling Rock heaven. I forgot how cheap it is to drink in Tennessee. I keep going to the bar and ordering rounds for everyone, as if I'm Mr. Moneybags, and not Mr. Unemployed. But honestly, the rate of the Tennessee dollar to the New York dollar must have changed drastically in the last few years. Suddenly, I'm wealthy.

"Remember your twenty-first birthday, Derek? Right before you deserted us for the Big City?" Kit dramatically exhales from her unlit cigarette and clutches my arm. "We came here for Animal Hour. They don't even have that anymore. Apparently it's now illegal to serve 3 for 1 drinks. Too many 'trustafarians' crashing their SUVs. Boring!"

Trustafarians was Kit's word for the trust fund hippies who extolled the virtues of Bob Marley while spending Daddy's hard earned money. Kit and I knew, and slept with, our fair share of them.

"What a crazy night!" I said. "Steve the bartender made us rainbow shooters. Red, orange, yellow, green, blue and violet. I remember the purple one was Grape Nehi and vodka. Epic. Didn't we break into that apartment complex on the hill and go skinny dipping?"

"Oh, you had such a crush on that straight boy," said Kit. "You made him come along. That frat boy. Whatshisname? Patrick Something the third. Everyone called him Trip, right?"

"God, Kit. Please bring up every failed conquest." I hid my face in my hands. "I'm not at my most wounded now, or anything. But honestly, I didn't *make* him do anything. That boy came willingly. Trust me." I grinned.

"Oh, hush!" she said. "If you didn't chase all the straight ones, we wouldn't have this problem, now would we?"

"Well, I learned my lesson with Trip," I reminded them. "He and I spent weeks together. I was in love. I was just too stupid to realize that Trip just liked getting blow jobs."

"Too much information." Tommy reached for his beer and laughed.

"You know I called him once?" I said. "Years later. He pretended that he didn't remember me."

"Why on *Earth* would you do that?" Bammy was not the emotional, hold-on-to-them type. She loved fast and hard, and if they ran, she turned her back and marched on to the next one.

"Ah, you know me," I said. "I'm emotional. I hold onto things, people, memories, experiences. I never let anyone go."

"Except for David," said Bammy, to the point, as always. "You let that one go. And he was far from straight. What happened?" She stared right at me, intensely.

"It wasn't right," I stammered. "It just... it wasn't right."

"But what about New York?" said Kit. "Aren't you afraid you'll be missing something? Missing out?"

"I'm not missing anything," I smiled. "Everything I need is right here."

And then, as if on cue, "Ring of Fire" filled the speakers, and everything I needed was indeed right there, including Johnny Cash.

4

UNCLE BARRY

Tommy followed me home in his car, just to make sure I made it safely. I had been living in the land of taxis and subways for so long that I had forgotten what it meant to have a few drinks and then need to get home on your own. I reminded myself to find a good car service for occasions like these. We journeyed down the back roads of my youth, and I felt that I knew them better than any roads I had ever traveled. Each twist and turn was comforting, and as we slowly made our way out west, I could feel that homing beacon pulling me towards the woods.

We pulled into Mom's driveway and Tommy and I stepped out of his car and into the headlights. "You gonna be all right, man?" he asked.

"Yeah, I'm fine. Thanks for following. I guess I forgot how stiff the pours were down South."

"You'll get used to it, again," he said. "There's no place like home, right Dorothy?"

"Really, dude? You went there?" I playfully punched him in the arm.

"Haha! It's good to have you back, Derek," he said. "We missed ya, man. We all love ya, you know that, right?"

"Shut up and get out of here before I kiss you," I laughed.

He threw me that Tommy smirk, tipped his forehead in a sign of respect and turned back to his car.

"I'll give you a call tomorrow after I see Bammy at the school," I called after him as I headed towards the house.

"You really think that's a good idea?" he asked. "Getting a job at the high school we graduated from?"

"Hey, I need a job," I said. "I may as well put that Theatre Arts major to work, since it didn't get much action in New York. And now that Miss B. has retired, well, there's a job opening. I promised Bammy that I'd consider it, at least. She can be damn convincing. Or maybe that was the whiskey talking." We both smiled as he shut his car door and he waved.

Tommy's headlights became small fireflies blinking in the distance as I stumbled towards the house and headed towards the side door. As a true Southern family, we never used the front door. That was reserved for salesmen, Christmas carolers, and other assorted strangers.

Mom left the light on for me in the kitchen, and as I crept towards the stairs I heard Uncle Barry call out in a stage whisper.

"Hey, Mr. New York City!" He smiled at me. "Get over here and let me take a look at you."

Barry was seated at the dining room table, cupping a glass of brandy in his hands. He always had a flair for the dramatic.

"Is that a kimono?" I asked.

"What, this?" He held one hand up and looked himself up and down. "This is a dressing gown, kid. Some of us still know how to look stylish, you know. You will most certainly never see 'Juicy' spelled out across this ass."

He stood up and gave me a real bear hug. He felt soft and cushy and smelled of aftershave. Barry had been a real looker in his day: dark wavy hair, a barrel chest, skinny waist and big, strong legs. Jeans cuffed just the right way, with sturdy brown boots. Blue eyes you could swim in and a smile that would set girls' hearts aflutter from fifty paces. Your average Tennessee Mountain Man. To hear my mom tell it, her younger brother was at the top of every girl's Homecoming list, but Janey was the one who lassoed him. The story goes she asked him out for the Sadie Hawkins' Dance their junior year, and the rest, as they say, is history. They were married straight out of high school.

"Well, look at you," he said, eyeing me up and down. "So damn skinny. Don't they feed you up in New York?"

"I've discovered the best diet, Uncle Barry," I said. "Vodka and being poor."

"Cheers to that!" and he raised his glass.

I pulled out a chair and sat next to him. "Mom said you were at a Bears' Club meeting. How's that going these days?" I asked.

"Well, I don't talk about it too much with Audrey. I don't think she's that interested. But tonight was very exciting. Very. I don't mean to brag," he said as he placed his brandy on the table and looked down, as if he were acting humble, "but you are looking at the newly elected Supreme Grizzly of The Bears' Club, local den 342." A smile spread across his face and I could see how proud he was.

"Congratulations! That's pretty cool." I clinked imaginary glasses with him, then stood up, walked in to the kitchen and grabbed a glass of water to dampen the impending hangover. "You need anything before I head up to bed?" I asked.

"No, I'm off to bed soon, too," he said. "It was a very full day. Elections for Supreme Grizzly and Grizzly Court. We promoted a few Cubs to Brown Bears and some Browns to Black. Very exciting stuff. But that's all I can say. Club secrets, you know," and he winked at me as he lifted his glass to his lips, once again.

"Of course, I said. "Lips sealed," and I made a show of locking them and throwing away the imaginary key.

"I want to hear all about your adventures, Derek. But not tonight. This Grizzly needs his beauty rest."

He stood up and pulled his dressing gown tight. I gave him a quick peck on the cheek and slowly padded up the stairs, glass of water in hand.

My mind was overthinking, as usual. That dressing gown really did look like a kimono, though. And cubs and bears? Did he even understand how that could be misconstrued? Now I know I've drunk too much. What I need is a good night's sleep.

After all, tomorrow I need to decide what to wear to school.

5

BACK TO SCHOOL

The alarm went off at 7:00 am, and I was sure it was a mistake. Memories of Bammy, Kit, Tommy and The Firelight trudged their way towards my few remaining brain cells, alongside the lovely aftertaste of beer and whiskey. Must get out of bed. Must do it. Now.

How stupid was I to get drunk the night before my big job interview? I guess I got caught up in the magic of being home, but it was a mistake I don't plan on making again. I need to take this job seriously.

A long hot shower can do a man wonders. Truly. I opened the bathroom door and popped back across the hall into my room. The contents of my suitcase had exploded across my old bedroom floor. Let's see, what's a respectable outfit for an interview as a high school theatre teacher? This felt too young, that too hip. All black feels so lovingly New York, but here it just comes across as Goth. Ah, yes. Here we go, the old stand by. Checked shirt and chinos. Should I wear a tie? I need to look respectable. I don't have a tie. Do I have a tie? Oh, crap.

I stepped out in the hall and noticed Barry had taken over the bathroom. "Barry," I yelled through the bathroom door, "I need to look in your room for a tie. Is that okay?"

All I heard was a few bars from "There Ain't Nothing Like a Dame" echoing from the shower stall, so I took that as a yes.

Let's see, where does Barry keep his ties? Dresser? Top drawer socks, second drawer underwear. Wow. Lots of silky things in here. He really kept a lot of Janey's bras. Maybe the closet? Dress shirts, trousers, dresses, more dresses. He really kept a lot of Janey's heels. I don't remember her having so many shoes, but then again, I didn't really pay attention. Barry, where are your ties? Don't you have a simple non-pattern... yes! This one will do.

I threw the noose around my neck, ran down the stairs and out the door, with one of Mom's homemade biscuits smeared with jelly in my hand. So much for my low carb, low sugar lifestyle. I really do need to start running regularly again and not just talk about it. I should go to the park at the lake this weekend.

I pulled into the school parking lot, and everything felt as strange as I imagined. After ten minutes of circling the senior lot looking for a spot, I realized I wasn't a senior anymore. My brain must have been on autopilot. I popped over to the visitors' lot and voila, front row.

I walked in through the front door and into the school office. "Good morning," I said. "I'm here to see the Vice Principal? Rebecca Talbot?"

"Derek Walter, you can call her Bammy 'round these parts, don't ya think?" Miss Mabel swung her chair around and took me in. "I'd recognize that voice blindfolded," she said. "You done spent the better part of your four years here up on that stage in the auditorium. And oh my, but you did grow up, didn't you?"

Miss Mabel had been my Aunt Janey's best friend. Even though she was older, they used to be inseparable. She had been the Parkville High School secretary since time began. Her hair was grayer now and pulled back into a low bun against her neck. She had swaddles of extra, loose skin, as if she was a Michelin Man who had spent a very long time in the sun and then suddenly deflated. It was rumored that she was at one time extremely overweight, and the ripples of skin were the result of a severe weight loss. When I went to Parkville High, it was also rumored that she was well into her sixties, which would place her in her late seventies or early eighties today. But she was not an easy one to figure out. We knew nothing about her personal life, but the "Miss" in front of her name told us more than enough. Either she was single by choice, or by accident. And very few people in the South are single by choice.

"She's a waitin' fer ya," Mabel said, pointing a crooked finger down towards the back hallway. "Just swing that gate open and head on down the hall. First office on the left."

"Thank you, Miss Mabel," I offered. "It's a pleasure seeing you again."

"Flattery will get you everywhere, young man. But not too far with me. I got too many other things to do." And with that she turned back to her computer.

The door was open, but I rapped on the frame lightly, as a sign of respect. Bammy was on the phone. She gave me that "one second" look with her eyes and pointed to a chair. I still couldn't get over the feeling that I was in the Vice Principal's office, as if I had gotten caught for something and I was about to be punished. Do we ever really outgrow the fears of high school?

"Yes, Mrs. Carter," Bammy said into the phone, nodding her head as if the recipient could actually see her. "Yes, Mrs. Carter. I'm afraid that's the decision, Mrs. Carter. Yes. One week suspension. No. No, that's not possible. There *is* no jury, Mrs. Carter. There is no appeal. This a decision we are sticking with. Mrs. Carter? Mrs. Carter." Her voice grew more stern. "No, it is not something we can just overlook. Chip exposed himself to the entire lunchroom, Mrs. Carter. Yes, I understand. Yes, boys will be boys, but Chip will have to sit this week out. I'm sorry you feel that way. I need to excuse myself now, I have an important meeting to attend. Yes, of course, your husband is welcome to call. No, ma'am. Yes, ma'am. No ma'am. You, too. Good day." And with that, she placed the phone back down on the receiver.

"What the what?" I asked.

"Bless her heart," she said, exasperated. "And believe me, Derek, Chip Carter is not the kind of guy anyone could overlook. Those freshman girls he exposed himself to are going to need a lot of counseling in their relationships if they expect their future husbands to be Chip Carter-sized, if you catch my drift."

"Oh, my…" I laughed.

"You have no idea." Bammy reached for her iced coffee and sucked on the straw, eyebrows raising.

"I was walking in here and I thought, 'When did all these kids suddenly look like adults?' Did we look like this?" I asked. "Because I remember feeling small and scrawny and immature and awkward. It looks like a boy band convention in a fancy gym out there! Those kids are styled. Like, they are ready for a photo shoot!"

"I have no clue," she said. "One day I was a French teacher, inspiring young minds to travel the world, and the next day we were invaded by catalogue models, rock stars and the fashion forward elite. Did you catch some of the athletes, by any chance? My god, I hope they don't ever test those boys for steroids. Lord, have mercy." She put her iced coffee down and rolled her eyes to the heavens.

"I blame the Internet," I said. "And porn. Unrealistic expectations. Years from now when the aliens invade they'll just laugh at us."

"I'd keep that to yourself in the interview, babe," she offered, wisely.

■ ■ ■

It turned out that my conversation with Principal Bellman was only a formality. Miss B., the former theatre teacher, was an institution at Parkville High School, having taught there for well over 40 years. The school year had just started that week, and Miss B.'s sudden decline in health dictated a swift retirement. Principal Bellman remembered me from years ago, and the conversation was over and done with before I realized it. Before I even had time to think, I accepted his offer of employment. In a few days I would start my new life as a high school teacher teaching acting and speech classes, as well as overseeing the Theatre Arts Club.

Bammy had warned me to not throw "the gay thing," as she called it, in his face. After so many years in New York, I refused to be closeted, but the topic never came up, and I didn't wave my rainbow flag. We have a very simple way of dealing with the subject of sexuality in the South. Basically, we don't deal with it at all.

We don't talk about it to our parents. We don't bring it up in church. We don't discuss it with our school counselors or elders. Honesty, we don't even really talk about it with our friends. And gay men never discuss it with their wives. Yes, you heard me right. Their wives. Southern men are expected to get married and have kids and attend church and be good, upstanding citizens, even if that means hiding the fact that you'd prefer to be Jim and Edward, rather than Jim and Edna. There were the occasional whispers and gossip. Of course we knew so-and-so preferred the company of men, but nary a word was spoken out loud, or anywhere where they could hear it, at least. It just wasn't polite.

"Let me give you a tour," said Bammy, leading me from the office. "Not that anything has really changed, but I'll show you the Teacher's Lounge and the private bathroom. Oh! And we have a new coffee machine. Exciting, isn't it? Not as good as your fancy New York espresso bars, but we take what we can get, right?" She pulled my hand and led the way through the halls, full of super jocks and models in expensive outfits, with the occasional academic overachiever trying to hide among the masses. Things hadn't changed that much, actually. In fact, my heart was pounding as if nothing had changed at all.

That's when I saw him, walking straight towards us. And suddenly, I could feel my sweat glands shooting jets of water under my arms, like a magical fountain in Las Vegas at midnight. But without the colored lights. At least, I hoped.

Luke Walcott. He had gone to school with Bammy and me. Captain of the football team. Captain of the track team. Captain of the swim team. Homecoming King, three years in a row.

Luke Walcott. Dirty blond hair, 6'2", blue eyes, and rugged jaw. A freakin' walking GI Joe. Voted Most Athletic, Most Popular, and Best Looking guy of my high school class.

Luke. The ultimate dream man of every female student in school, and a few of the guys, too.

Fucking Luke. I hated him.

"Derek, do you remember Luke Walcott?" Bammy asked me. "Luke, I'm not sure you remember Derek Walter. Derek is joining us as our new theatre teacher, replacing Miss B. Luke is our Head Coach for football and track." And she just stood there, smiling.

Did I remember Luke Walcott? Is she fucking kidding me?! Bammy, how have you suddenly forgotten entire chunks of our friendship? Has the vodka finally eaten your brain? Ah, yes. That's right. I've been out of the game too long. We're being "Southern." We are ignoring the unfortunate moments in our youth that make it uncomfortable when meeting again as adults. I had completely forgotten some of these games. It was high time I brought myself up to speed.

Well, yes Bammy, I do remember Luke Walcott. Unfortunately. How could I forget? He terrorized me, ever since he transferred here in eighth grade from Savannah. I remember the day he arrived as the new kid in class. Always the same. They start off nice, charming, and friendly to everyone. Making their way through the herd, calculating the best path to super stardom. Popularity is everything when you are twelve. Within a week, he was in with the jocks and cheerleaders. After a month, he was their king. By the time we were in high school, he was the supreme leader over everyone athletic and good-looking. One approving nod from him and you were golden. A smirk? You were toast.

And me? *Best. Toast. Ever.* Elbowed into lockers, tackled mercilessly during flag football, thrown into the showers fully clothed, all to the growing cheers of my fellow inmates. And not just once. Repeatedly.

It wasn't because I was gay. No, we didn't mention that. Kids are far too simplistic for that, actually. It was simply because I just didn't fit in. I didn't fit with the "fits," and I didn't fit with the "misfits." And people like Luke Walcott demanded that the weak be devoured. Survival of the fittest, in action.

"Derek, was it?" he said. "Hi. Nice to see you. Welcome." Luke extended his hand to shake mine. I froze for a second. All those years. All that torment, and here I am faced with the moment where I can finally say what I have been wanting to say to him for years. It's not like I practiced it in a mirror about a million times, or anything, but here goes. Get ready, Luke. I hope you're prepared for this onslaught, because here it comes, Big Man on Campus!

"Nice to see you, as well," I said and extended my hand, smiles all around.

Pardon me. Has anyone seen my balls? I seem to have misplaced them.

6

THE LUNCH ROOM

A high school cafeteria is the perfect setting for a reality show. And a shoot out.

Week one was over, and I was getting settled into my new role. Bammy and I carried our trays towards the teachers' tables and found a spot near the end. It felt very strange to be sharing a space with so many of the blue hairs who had left their indelible prints on the psyche of my youth. Mrs. Miller's fingers and tongue were still blue and green from the dry erase markers she used on the overhead projector in her geometry class. Good to see that some things haven't changed. At all.

"How does it feel so far?" asked Bammy. "Weird, right? That'll pass." She was focused on deconstructing a slice of pizza from the school cafeteria, carefully pulling the cheese and pepperoni off the soggy bread underneath.

"I had forgotten how much fun it was to drink chocolate milk from one of these tiny cardboard boxes," I said, trying desperately to open the spout without destroying the entire carton. These things are definitely not made for adult fingers and thumbs.

"So," she ventured, "did I notice a bit of tension between you and Luke Walcott last week when we had our tour? What's up with that?" She scooped some pizza cheese onto her fork and started eating, oblivious to the verbal dogs I was about to unleash.

"Bammy, are you kidding me?" I said. "That guy tortured me when we were kids. I had nightmares about coming to school, I was so freaked out about what his gang of followers would do to me."

"Honestly," she said, putting her fork down and reaching for her diet soda, "I don't remember it being that bad. Yeah, kids are jerks, but are you sure you're remembering it right?" She looked at me with raised eyebrows and took another sip.

"Bammy, you were much more popular than me. I mean, we were friends and all, but we kind of ran in different circles," I said, frustrated that our memories could be so different. "You hung out with all those pretty girls and I was hanging with the drama geeks and band nerds. Maybe I didn't confide in you as much back then," I conceded, "but I'm not making up how it felt to see him again. I felt like a teenager, and I hated it." I couldn't be that angry with her. I loved Bammy, and I needed every friend I could get right now, but our memories on this subject were not agreeing.

"Mind if I join you?" The voice came from above. I looked up and saw Luke, decked out in his coach shorts and whistle, his pectoral muscles desperately trying to escape the confines of his Tennessee Volunteers t-shirt. My god, this man was... my enemy. Concentrate, Derek!

"Uh," I stared at his chest and looked up into his stark blue eyes, unsure of what to say. Why is he here? Can't he sit with the prison guards?

Bammy caught my gaze, wrinkled her brow and gave me that *what the hell is wrong with you?* look. "Not at all! Grab a seat," she offered, trying to overcome my awkwardness and casting a firm *be nice!* glance my way.

"Great, thanks." He grinned and took the seat next to me and placed his tray down: two cheeseburgers, a side salad and two cartons of whole milk. "So, how's your first week been?" He looked over at me with the kind of smile that dentists place in ads on the subway to attract guys like me. And dimples. Did he always have these perfect dimples? I don't remember those.

"Uh, fine." I looked down at my salad, breaking eye contact. The last thing I wanted to do was talk to Luke Walcott. I speared a carrot stick and shoved it in my mouth, casually staring towards the windows, hoping in my mind that he would go away. How do I end up in these situations?

"I'm sure you'll do great here," he said, picking up a cheeseburger. "Miss B. is a tough act to follow, but the school could use some young blood." He took a bite, then looked at me, thoughtfully. "Say, I've been wracking my brain, did we know each other in high school? When did you graduate?" His blue eyes looked straight at me, with no recognition.

My god. Is this really happening to me? Him, too? How could he possibly not remember me? Was I really so invisible in high school?

"Um, yeah," I sputtered. "Well, we did know each other. We didn't exactly run in the same circles, but yeah, we actually graduated together in the same class." I could feel my heart pounding in my chest. I felt like one of those kidnap victims finally confronting his captor, years later.

"Really? Wow," he said. "I mean, I kind of remember you doing plays and things, but I don't think we actually spoke too much, if ever. Did we?"

"Not if you don't count me screaming and begging for you to not throw me in the showers after gym class." I did it. Be brave, Derek. Stand up for yourself!

"Wait, what?" he placed his cheeseburger down on his plate and focused his eyes intently upon me. He actually looked hurt, as if I had wounded him.

"Oh, come on, Luke," I said, my anger cresting. "Don't play that shit. Sorry, but this is a stupid charade. You were a total *dick* to me!" I lost it. "How could you possibly forget that? You tormented me!" I stared at him and I could tell I may have gone too far. Was I acting like a crazy man?

Luke looked at me as if I had just shot his favorite puppy. He raised his eyebrows and took a deep breath. "Whoa. Listen, buddy… I don't remember that. But really, I'm sorry if I was a jerk. Kids are stupid, and I definitely did a lot stupid things that I am not proud of. I got caught up in the popularity hustle. But if I did something to hurt you, well, I'm sorry, man. Really I am." His words rang true, and I felt so confused.

My heart was pounding, my mind was racing, and no words were forming in my brain. I was staring at Luke, dumbfounded. How could something that was so traumatic to me be so inconsequential to him that he actually forgot it?

"Listen… I should probably get going," said Luke, knowing when to cut and run. "We're running extra practices leading up to the big Homecoming game. You two enjoy your lunch, now, hear?" And with that, he picked up his lunch and lumbered slowly towards the tray return. He didn't look back, and I started to regret my outbreak.

"Whoa. Intense shit." Bammy broke the silence. "You okay?"

"How many more classes until beer o'clock?" I asked. I'd just confronted a demon from my childhood, and it turns out that not only does he not remember being a demon, but he may actually not be a bad guy. Was the demon mainly in my head? Were my memories wrong? Did I blow it all out of proportion? I was so confused, I didn't know what to think or feel or believe. I know that when I woke up this morning, Luke Walcott was the enemy. Now, I wasn't so sure.

And damn. Those dimples.

■ ■ ■

The following week it was pouring rain as I stepped from the car and ran as fast I as could towards the doors of the school, hopping over puddles like a long jumper. The sun was shining brightly, but the skies were opening up above as if Noah himself should clearly take note. When I was a kid I loved rainy days in the South. Mom and I used to sit on the front porch and watch the sky pour down over the neighborhood, listening to the thunderclouds as they retreated or advanced, counting the seconds between the booms of thunder and the flashes of lightning to determine the distance. I used to love to sit out in the street at the curb, legs splayed, the warm rain pouring over me like a bathtub on the pavement.

Today, I was just thinking about my shoes. Funny how our priorities change as we get older. And gayer.

The day passed without a Luke sighting. I had mixed emotions after our lunchroom confrontation the week before. Truthfully, I felt like an ass. I mean, I know that deep down I had the right to feel like I did, but maybe I should just get over it. We were kids. Perhaps I colored the memories, making him out to be much worse than he was? Did I just fixate on him? Why not the other guys who were involved? And he couldn't possibly know what I was going through as a kid, dealing with my parents splitting up, my same sex attractions, my overall awkwardness. *Ugh*. It sucks being an adult.

Classes came and went without much thought. After years of working with the various theatre workshop kids in New York, this was a breeze. I had put up a flyer on the bulletin board, the school newspaper and our website for auditions for our first show. We were meeting today after school, in the theatre. Ready for the biggest cliché ever? I chose *Grease* as our fall musical. What can I say? Pre-questionable sexuality John Travolta still pushed all the right buttons for me.

I walked outside the main building and under the covered walkway towards the theatre. Imagine my surprise when

I unlocked the door to find that it was raining. Inside. On the stage! And no, this was not some exciting music video being filmed at our school.

"Oh, shit!" I said.

"*Ooooh*, Mr. Walter, just cussed!" Kids. Behind me, waiting to get in. I forgot there were kids present. Crap.

"Never mind me. *And just forget I said that.* What the heck? We can't have auditions if it's raining inside," I said to them. I had no idea what to do, where to go. "I know you kids are excited and have prepared for this, but maybe we should postpone the auditions."

"Well," offered one of my students, "we could go over to the gym? There's a piano over there, too." Out of the mouths of babes. Brilliant!

"And that's why they pay you the big bucks," I said, quizzical looks all around. I needed to surround myself with a better audience. "Let's go, kids."

We made a quick pit stop in the office to alert Miss Mabel about the leak in the auditorium. She called Maintenance, but they wouldn't be able to do anything right away, so I marched my merry band of misfits over to the gym, flung open the doors and *boom!* A football came flying towards me and landed in my arms, scooped up like a little baby.

Luke jogged over, sheepish grin on his face. "Hey, Mr. Walter. Sorry about that." His hands were placed on his hips in the classic coach stance. "Nice catch, though! Where'd you learn to do that?"

"We're not all Marcia Brady, you know," I jeered, and tossed the pigskin back to him, with as much force as I could muster.

He caught it smoothly, of course, pulled it in, a slight smile on his face.

"I can see that. What can I do ya for?" he said. Does he always have to be so nice?

"Well, we were hoping to use the piano. The theatre seems to have sprung a leak, and we're planning on auditioning for *Grease*, not *Singing in the Rain*. We thought maybe we could use the gym." I peered around, but could see that my case was about to be dismissed. The floor was full of sweaty teens covered in shoulder pads and protective helmets, running from one end of the floor to the other.

"Ah, well, we had to bring practice inside today," he explained. "The field became a mud swamp, and I can't afford for any of my players to get injured before the big Homecoming game. We have to beat Billington, ya know." That grin. White teeth. Those dimples. God, he is making it awfully hard to hate him.

"Well, kids, it looks like Coach Walcott doesn't care about your dreams," I said, turning to my flock. "Auditions are postponed to Monday. Sorry. Hopefully our auditorium will be back in shape by then."

Luke looked at me slightly anxiously, as if I had wounded him unnecessarily, again. He then turned back to his team, football in hand. Damn it. I can really be an ass.

7

ONE MORE, ON ME

After my latest run in with Luke, I was looking forward to meeting the Scooby Gang at The Firelight tonight.

I raced home for a quick shower. Mom left a note on the fridge along with a peach cobbler she had whipped up on the counter. Uncle Barry was at his club and she was out with her girlfriends. I was convinced that she was trying to fatten me up so that I would never have a social life again and I would spend more time with her. I made a quick costume change, checked my look in the mirror, and hopped down the stairs, practically tripping over myself. I had a goal, of course. I wanted to get to Happy Hour before it ended.

And… shit. The car won't start. When I showed up on Mom's doorstep after leaving my boyfriend, my city and my life, I didn't exactly have the cash on hand for a new set of wheels. Luckily, mom still had her old car parked behind the house, but it needed a little work. Her 1978 baby blue Buick Regal with the "Honk if You Love Willie Nelson" bumper sticker had seen plenty of adventures (and honks) during my lifetime, but it was time to bring him back into service. We put just enough money into him to make him run, but I guess it wasn't enough.

Click. Click. Click. Nada.

I called Tommy. "Hey, it's me. Willie Nelson's dead," I said. "Can you swing by and pick me up on your way to The Firelight?"

"No problem, man," he said. "I'm on my way." That's Tommy. He'll show up for you in a heartbeat, and just expect a smile in return, no questions asked.

I walked down to the end of the driveway and waited for him by the mailbox. I absentmindedly looked at my phone and checked my e-mail and text messages. Not a word from David since I left New York. I hoped he was doing okay, but truthfully, I didn't want to hear from him just yet. I knew Marcos and his other friends would check in on him, but I wasn't ready to take that step, myself. I imagined he hated me. I would. But I was dreading the moment when our Wall of Silence would inevitably come crashing down and I would have to deal with the repercussions of my decisions.

Tommy pulled up and I jumped in the passenger seat. "Thanks, man," I said and reached over, giving him a one-armed half hug. "Really sorry about that."

"All good! I'm glad to spend some time with you," he said.

"So, how are things? How's the family?" I asked.

"Ah, you know," he said. "Everyone's crazy but we don't really deal with it." He took a drag off his cigarette and flicked it out the window.

"Welcome to my trailer park," I agreed, and we laughed. I knew all too well what life was like in a Southern family. We keep our loved ones in the attic, the basement, or the closet. Literally.

We pulled into The Firelight and found a parking spot up front. Bammy and Kit had both sent text messages to say that they were already there and had scored our regular booth. Tommy and I walked up the steps and into the bar to the strains of "Blister in the Sun" blaring from the jukebox, and sure enough, the ladies had their pitchers propped in front of them at the wide circular booth in the back, but it seems their text messages only told half the story. Yes, they had saved seats for me and Tommy, but it turned out they were sharing the booth with three others; Scooter Lee, Tammy Jeffries, and... Luke Walcott. Seriously?!

"Hey, y'all," I said, trying to act cool. But even I could tell I was faking it. I do not have a poker face. At all. Luke barely registered my presence, which only pissed me off more. He was too busy talking to Tammy's breasts, pushed up and out for the world's approval.

"There you go with the 'y'alls' again," Tommy snickered. "You just pull those out in front of a crowd to prove your Southern street cred, right?" Laughs all around, at my expense.

"Fuck *all y'all*," I said, pointedly, and smiled. "Now, where's my drink?"

Tommy and I scooted in next to Kit and Bammy. Kit was decked out in her best Audrey Hepburn *Funny Face* get up, complete with French beret. Bammy had on a cashmere sweater with an embroidered crest. How I was able to pull this group of friends together, I will never know, but I was sure grateful for their friendship.

"Hey there, Derek. Welcome back." Scooter offered up his beer for a toast. Scooter Lee and I had never really talked that much in high school. He didn't run with the jocks or the popular kids, so I wasn't sure why Luke was hanging with him and Tammy. Scooter was pure redneck, and proud of it.

"I been followin' you on Instagram, you know," said Tammy. "I bet you got all kinds of stories for us about New York City." From the way she was basically in his lap, I figured that Tammy and Scooter were still an item. They looked good together, actually.

"Ah, well, I loved New York, but it was time to come home," I said, gripping my beer. "I missed my fiends, my family. You know." I also loved avoiding discussing David in Tennessee. Too much drama, too much gay. Few people went there.

"Not really. None of us have traveled like you have," she said, one arm on Scooter's leg, another holding her pint glass. "We ain't had the opportunity. I lead more of a 'white trash' kinda life." She giggled.

We all laughed. It wasn't really a derogatory thing if you said it about yourself.

"Exactly how white trash are you?" said our resident southern belle, Bammy, playing into the joke.

"Third generation trailer park," said Tammy proudly.

"Wow. That's impressive," I offered, glass raised.

"Thanks," she said. "The men kept movin' on, but we kept the house. Though a few of Mama's boyfriends did try to take it. It's on wheels, after all."

Pitchers were emptied and new rounds bought. The juke-box offered up scores of the best of Country and Indie Pop, and the conversation flowed. Every now and then I'd catch Luke glancing at me, but overall he was hanging with Scooter and Tammy, while my friends and I caught up in our end of the booth. No drama so far, and I was fine with that. I wasn't sure what this tension was, but I was beginning to feel I owed him an apology for tearing into him at the lunchroom table my first week at school. I just wasn't looking forward to starting that conversation. I do not eat crow well.

Kit was telling us about how she met her boyfriend Shawn, her Guitar Hero. "He was playing bass one night at The Bongo Room with his 80s cover band, Shock the Monkey, and we kinda made eyes at each other during this really bad Phil Collins med-ley. We ended up talking a bit during their break, but nothing really came of it. I kept seeing him around town, but it's like he was afraid to approach me. Then I found out he was talking about me, and not in a good way. I totally would have slept with him if he hadn't already told all his friends that I had slept with him, you know? Anyway, I made up my mind that he was a total jerk, so I just ignored him. A lot. And don't you know it? A few weeks later there he was, tail between his legs, flowers in hand. Y'all know I'm a sucker for flowers. And now he's trained!" They had been together for over a year now, and she seemed brighter and prettier than I had ever seen her. I was really happy for her.

"Well, you seem to have found *the one*," said Bammy. "And Tommy seems pretty serious with his new girlfriend, Meredith. Let's hope there are a few princes left for me and Derek." With that, we emptied our glasses and set them down on the table.

"Who's got the next round? I lost count," I said.

"Sorry, guys, I'm out. Today was a killer, and I just want my couch, a movie and my cat," said Bammy.

"Me, too," said Kit. "Sorry. Not the couch and the cat, but Shawn is playing a late set tonight at The Bongo Room and I need to play the part of 'Hopeless Groupie #1.' It makes him happy, and the happier he is, the more presents for me." She clapped her hands with glee and we all smiled.

"Well, Tommy, I guess that leaves you and me," I said, and stood up to give the girls a kiss and turned to head towards the bar.

But Tommy stood up, too. "Sorry, man. Meredith just sent a text message. Duty calls. You mind if I take you back to your mom's place now?"

A voice spoke up. "I can drive him back." We all turned our heads towards the other end of the table. "Your mom lives out west, down by the lake, right?" said Luke.

"Uh, yeah. She does. But…" I didn't know what to say.

"No, really, it's no problem. I got ya." He looked up at me with those baby blues and set his empty glass down. "One more round? It's on me."

Expect the unexpected, right?

■ ■ ■

My Scooby Gang deserted me, and Scooter and Tammy said their good-byes, as well. Scooter was a mechanic and he had an early shift at the auto repair shop, and Tammy needed to rest up for her full night tomorrow. She was pulling a double at Chesty Cheese.

Luke headed to the bar and I sat in the booth, watching him from behind. Or rather, watching his behind. My god. That man did not skip leg day at the gym.

Luke turned and made a beeline towards the booth, a full pitcher and two fresh glasses in hand. He darted in and out of the crowd, deftly avoiding any other bodies, running interference like the good football player that he was. He slid into the booth next to me, grinning, placed the pitcher down and poured two perfect pints.

"Cheers," he said, straight white teeth and soft laugh lines at the corners of his eyes. What the hell is going on? I have no idea. Just go with it, right?

"Cheers," I offered back, glass raised, never breaking eye contact. We drank. Glasses down. And then the silence. Followed by silence. And more long, uncomfortable silence. My god, someone has to give…

"So, listen," I began. "I really wanted to say…" and before I can even get my apology going, he starts talking.

"Derek, sorry for interrupting," he said "but something's been bugging me. I just need to get this off my chest, man." He looked over at me, and I couldn't refuse. He had my attention.

"And what a chest it is." Damn it, Derek. I always fall back on humor to break the ice.

He smiled, softly. "Seriously. I've been thinking a lot about what you said during lunch last week."

I looked down, swallowed meekly, then back up into his eyes. My teeth gnashed and I tightened my jaw. Where the hell is he going with this?

"I don't really remember things the way you did," he started, "but that doesn't mean that I didn't do some stupid things that may have hurt you. I don't know if you know or not, but I had a classic Southern family: all good on the surface, but really messed up on the inside. I didn't really talk about it to anyone, well, because I didn't really have anyone to talk to. You see, my mother died right before high school started. Breast cancer. So I was raised by my father and our housemaid for a few years, and well, it was kinda rough. Tough love and all that. He did his best. Anyway, that's not an excuse, just an explanation. Rosa had been with us since I was a kid. Our mother hired her to help out with my younger sister, Lana and me. Rosa was pretty amazing. Still is. But this isn't about that. What I did, I did, and if the man I am today could go back in time and change the way I acted as a kid, I would do it. Because I think you're a cool guy, Derek. I really do. I'm sorry. Truthfully, I am." He reached an arm up and placed a strong hand on my shoulder, squeezing softly.

I swallowed hard and looked deep into his eyes. He was being honest, or at least it felt that way to me.

"I don't know what to say," I said.

"Accept my apology?" he said. Those eyes. That smile.

"Of course, and I wanted to apologize, too, for jumping all over you in the lunchroom," I sputtered. "That was just way out of line and way out of proportion. I guess I had just built up this…"

"Water under the bridge," and he squeezed my shoulder again. "Let's start fresh?"

"Sure." I smiled, paused. "Hi, my name is Derek," and I held out my hand.

"Hi. I'm Luke. Nice to meet you."

Firm handshakes, and we both grinned.

We spent the rest of the night "shooting the shit." Nothing major, nothing tense, and nothing out of line. It seems Luke had evolved a lot since the days spent under his dad's thumb, and we had a few good laughs. Before we knew it, "Closing Time" was queued up on the jukebox, and we all made our way towards the exit and the parking lot.

"You sure you're all right to drive?" I asked.

"This good ole boy knows his way down a back road or two," he said as he unlocked the passenger side of his black Jeep Wrangler and held the door for me. "Ladies first."

"Asshole." I smirked.

"You love it." He smiled.

"Whatever." But I did. God help me, I did. What the fuck? Am I really flirting with Luke Walcott? Big Man On Campus, Luke Walcott? Homecoming King, Luke Walcott? Captain of the football team? How on Earth do I end up in these situations?

I crawled up into the leather seat, reached over and unlocked his door and put on my safety belt. The interior of the car smelled of leather and wood. No Polo cologne, thank God. So Luke wasn't 100% frat boy, after all?

He turned the radio on to the local college indie station, and we pretty much drove in silence. I know he was concentrating on the road and the turns, but I was concentrating on his strong right hand as he shifted gears, the vein in his arm pulsing. My jeans were feeling awfully tight, and I had to readjust a bit.

"Everything all right over there?" he smirked.

"All good," I said, remembering to act sober. "Just keep your eyes on the road and we'll be fine. Next left, then straight on down past the marina. You'll see a big barn up on the right, and it's the green mailbox on the left, just after that."

He pulled into Mom's driveway and stepped out, engine running, headlights on. He then walked in front of the car and over to my door, my eyes following him as I unbuckled my seat belt.

"Home, sir, as promised," he said, opening my door, other hand outstretched as if to lead the way.

I stepped out and he closed the door behind me. I turned, and before I could speak or think of what to do or say, he pulled me into his arms and held me there, tight, my head on his shoulder, just inches from his neck. My god he smelled good: smoky, almost like wood, as if he had slept the night downwind from a campfire.

"I had a great time," he said, over my shoulder. "Thanks for hanging with me." His strong arms held me there, for a second longer than a friend should. One second more, in fact, and I was about to give in, give up, and surrender. I felt my knees weaken and my own hands started to explore the muscles in his back...

Then he pushed himself away, firmly. He held one hand on the back of my neck and another at my waist and looked me deeply in the eyes.

"I'm actually a good guy, ya know?" he said.

"I can see that." I smiled, dumbfounded.

"Good night, buddy. Sleep tight." He patted me twice on the back, walked back over to the driver's side, jumped in and reversed out of the driveway, leaving me in the headlights, wondering what the hell just happened.

Good night...buddy?

8

HELLO, DOLLY

As I had promised myself, I went for a run by the lake Saturday morning to clear my thoughts. It didn't really work. Luke Walcott, what the hell are you doing in my head, and am I crazy? Readjusting to life in Tennessee was hard enough, but dealing with yet another crush on an unattainable straight boy was something I just didn't think I could go through right now. I had had enough heartbreak this year. It was time to just concentrate on my friends, my family, and me and have some fun.

The towing service came by and hauled Willie Nelson off to Scooter's shop for repairs. Kit picked me up at noon and we headed to The Tater Tot for lunch. One huge plate of cheese fries later and I was in carb heaven. All the worries and stresses of the last few weeks departed my body.

"My friend, this is better than any spa I've ever been to," I said, as that potato-filled cheese covered fork made its way towards my gaping pie hole.

"Comfort food is one thing," she said, "but real life bacon and cheese covered Southern comfort food is just a whole 'nother level. *Come. To. Mama!*" She dug into her fried potato skins with two hands.

We may ignore a lot of the uncomfortable conversations and subjects in the South, but one thing we do not ignore is the value of food as a binding source of love and friendship. And the food at The Tater Tot was definitely doing its job.

"Okay, Mister." Kit pushed her plate away and took a big swig of sweet ice tea. "The carbs are loaded and our energy reserves are in place. Let's get to the important task of the day. Thrifting!"

Kit was a wiz at finding cultural gems in the strangest of places. She knew every Goodwill, Salvation Army and Thrifty Bee from one end of town to the other. She had an uncanny ability to walk into a thrift store, junk shop or garage sale and find the one item that she could buy for five dollars and turn around and sell on eBay for two hundred. Vintage fiberglass Knoll chairs, George Nelson lamps, or Massimo Vignelli for Heller, Kit could spot them faster, see their value, and flip them for a profit better than anyone else. If I had been a gold miner in the Old West, I would have wanted Kit at my side.

We spent a few hours rummaging through junk and treasures. I felt dirty, but I was having a blast. Scooter called my cell phone in the late afternoon to say that Willie was alive and kicking again, so Kit dropped me off to pick up the car, and I headed home with a few old Brownie cameras to add to my mom's ever expanding collection of stuff.

Mom was in the kitchen making dinner when I walked in, and the house was filled with the smell of chicken fried steak, mashed potatoes, gravy and creamed spinach. I was in heaven, but honestly, I was beginning to worry that at this rate my high metabolism wouldn't hold out for too many more months, let alone years. The running was sure to help, but age certainly has a way of sneaking up on you.

"Plans tonight, honey?" Mom said, as she seasoned the gravy. She was wearing her apron, hunched over the stove, as I always pictured her, long wooden spoon in hand.

"Oh, just a quiet night. I'm heading over to Tommy's to watch a movie with him and his new girlfriend, Meredith. You know the drill. Third wheel strikes again. You?"

"Just dinner with you, then a long bubble bath and an early night," she said, pulling the chicken fried steaks from her cast iron skillet and plating our meal. "Barry's down at The Bears' Club. They are having some kind of performance tonight. I'm glad he has something he loves to occupy his time now that Janey's passed. It keeps him busy."

We ate dinner and caught up on my transition to my new life, so far. I told her about Bammy, Kit and Tommy and about my new job. We talked about my students, and the adjustments of living back in the South again after having spent so many years in New York. We didn't talk about David, though, and we certainly didn't talk about Luke. I know that my mom loves me unconditionally, but a parent cannot help but want what's best for their children, and I had a feeling that Mom knew David was not the best for me, but she had always been too sweet to say anything too harsh, so we avoided the topic altogether. I just didn't want to hear it. And I wasn't about to bring up yet another straight boy crush story. I'd had too many of those in my twenties, and they all ended in heartache.

I helped her clear the table, load the dishwasher and put away the few remaining leftovers. Chicken fried steak is always better the next day for lunch. The phone rang and she walked over to pick it up.

"Hello? Hi, there." It was obviously someone she knew on the other end of the line, as I could hear the smile in her voice. "What's that? Now, where upstairs? Sure thing. No problem. We just finished dinner so I can be there in about 15-20 minutes. Sounds good. Love ya, too. Bye," and she hung up the wall phone. Who still has a landline? My mom.

"What's up?" I asked.

"Oh, that was Barry. He forgot something in his room and needs me to drop it off for one of his performers."

"Well, I'm on my way to Tommy's," I offered. "I can drop off whatever he needs, if you want."

"Are you sure, honey?" She looked a bit tired, as if she could really use a good warm soak in the tub. "I don't want to keep you from your friends."

"Not at all. What is it?" I asked.

"Oh, he forgot a pair of earrings. They're having some big to-do tonight, and the star of the show needs a fancy pair of diamond something-or-others. They're Janey's. I'll go get them off his dresser." She headed upstairs and I walked over to the door and picked up my keys from the old wooden cigar box on the table.

She came down and I took the jewelry bag. Scooter had done a great job, and Willie started purring (with only a few minor rattles) before I was on the road, again. The Bears' Club was located downtown, not far from the college campus, but not too far from the "wrong side of the tracks." Downtown Parkville was a lot different when the club was founded, and today it was an odd location for what I assumed was a private gathering space for well-to-do members of our little town, but then again, I didn't know too much about The Bears. No one knew much more than they wanted you to know, actually.

Founded by Commodore William Parker soon after the Civil War, The Bears' Club had a long, splendid history as the "Premiere Gentleman's Club" of Parkville, attracting many of the Founding Fathers of our town. Mayors, Governors and even a former Vice President were members, at one time. No ladies were admitted, of course. In my mind's eye I imagined that it was filled with heavy mahogany card tables and leather banquettes, ready for thrilling nights of poker tournaments, whiskey drinking, cigars and political rumblings, so I was a bit excited to finally see inside. If they'd let me in, of course.

I pulled the car into the parking lot and walked towards the front door. I imagined there would be a secret knock or a tiny window, like at a speakeasy in a 1930's gangster film, but there was no such thing. In fact, the door was simply locked, with an engraved brass Members Only sign attached. No matter how many times I knocked, no one answered. Mom had told me that whenever she had dropped something off before, she just knocked, a hand reached out, and that was that. I could barely make out the sound of music behind the heavy oak door, so I could only assume the show had started and no one was manning the front. I hoped I wasn't too late.

Having worked in my fair share of restaurants, I knew there had to be a back entrance, so I made my way around the corner. The music grew louder as I passed through the hedge, and I saw a bit of light peaking through a bright red lacquered doorframe. I tried the handle and voila! It turned.

Feeling a bit like a kid who knew he was about to sneak through his parents' dresser drawers, I walked in to see that I was at the back entrance of what appeared to be a stage. I could hear music and laughter... and Donna Summer?

There was a large woman in front of me in a silver, sparkling beaded gown. She had her back turned to me, and her jet-black hair piled on top of her head in a great big bun, highlighted with a large fascinator hat that appeared to be accentuated with ostrich feathers. She was swaying slightly in her high heels to the music that was coming from onstage.

"*Ahem,*" I cleared my throat. "Excuse me, ma'am. I'm looking for Barry Henry?" I said.

She seemed to stiffen her back a bit, then turned slowly to face me.

"Well, hello Dolly," said my uncle Barry. And I dropped the jewelry bag on the floor.

9

THE PRICE OF ADMISSION

"Barry?" I asked.

"*Beret*, honey. In here, it's Beret," he said.

"But... what? I don't..." I was speechless.

"Well, it's sort of an homage to our love of all things French. And it's better than Ethel. I've learned a few tricks over the years. Listen kid, I love ya and I know you've got a million questions, but I've got a show to put on. Now that the cat's out of the closet, so to speak, you may as well stay and watch. Just stand over there by Scotty, the sound guy, and then you and I can have a heart-to-heart after I'm done. Now *do* be a dear and bend down for those rocks. They complete my outfit. I would do it, but this gown's too damn tight."

He (she?) batted his (her?) smoky grey eyelids at me as I knelt down to retrieve the jewelry bag at my feet. Beret quickly put the dangling diamond strands in her ears, gave me a *how do*

I look? look, hands framing her face, then turned on her heels towards the stage.

"Break a leg?" I said, as my uncle sashayed away, his/her sparkly covered ass swaying from side to side.

"Your first time?" said Scotty. He was standing in the corner with a clipboard in his hands.

"At a drag show? No. At a family drag show? Yes."

"Well, you're in for a treat," he said. "There's no one better in town than Beret."

Scotty was right. Beret was, in a word, priceless. She brought the house down with a rousing rendition of "Diamonds Are Forever," by Shirley Bassey, and exited to thunderous applause.

"Come on, kid," Beret said, walking offstage towards me after her number was over. "Let's head down to the dressing rooms. I think you and I have some catching up to do. Scotty? Be a doll and send us down a few vodka martinis, very dry. On second thought, make that a pitcher. And tell Ricky not to use the cheap shit. We're entertaining family."

With that, Beret grabbed my hand and we walked towards a staircase off stage right.

We headed below the building and entered a short hallway. It was warmly lit, but nowhere near as stately and hallowed as I imagined The Bears' Club to be. In fact, it looked a bit like this part of the building had undergone a not-so-successful renovation in the 1970s, with thick caramel shag carpeting and wood paneled walls.

Beret sat in front of a dressing room mirror and pointed to a chair and said "So, where do I begin?" she said. "I guess we have a bit more in common than you thought, huh?"

"Um, yeah. I mean, wow. I'm kind of thrown right now."
I was shocked, but not in a bad way. This revelation actually
made a lot of things make more sense to me. "I mean, I guess it
was right in front of me my whole life, but I never put two and
two together."

"Well, you *are* Southern," she said, removing her hat and
placing it to her right. "It's just polite to ignore that which stares
us plainly in the face. It's how we deal." Scotty knocked on
the doorframe and brought in a tray with a pitcher of vodka,
chilled, two highball glasses and some ice.

"Thanks, Scotty," said Beret. "Do be a sweetie and close
that door on your way out?" She filled the two martini glasses.
"Olives or twist?"

"Olives" I said. "Always."

"Two for good measure. Cheers, nephew!"

I gulped once. Twice. It was strange to take all of this in.
"You look like Mom, but in drag."

"Oh, please." Beret rolled her eyes and threw me shade.
"Your mother never could do a smoky eye. She does have better
tits, though."

"HA!" I coughed up vodka and covered my mouth in
shock. Beret just laughed at me and set her martini glass down.

"Barry? Sorry. *Beret.* Very French. Did Aunt Janey know?"
I asked.

"Oh, honey, who do you think taught me how to do a
smoky eye?" She set her glass down and looked at me, lovingly.
"Of course she did. I loved your Aunt Janey. Don't you dare
think otherwise. She was the love of my life. But we had an arrangement, and we both understood it. You and I come from

different generations, you know. You, we knew you were gay by the time you were four years old, but no one ever said anything. We just didn't. We didn't even talk about it before you moved to New York, but I could clearly see why you needed to leave. And you blossomed there, and really discovered yourself, and I'm proud of you. Kids nowadays are 'out' at twelve years old, and it's easy for them. I don't understand it. I'm jealous, of course, but it's just not the world I come from, and it wouldn't have been right for me, or you, for that matter. Janey and I met in high school, as you know. We dated, kissed, the whole thing. But more often than not, our kissing would lead to us laughing at how ridiculous we both felt. We were putting on an act, both of us. She was my best friend and I loved her, and I spent the best years of my life with her, and I don't regret a single minute of it. Neither did she."

"So, those clothes in your closet?" I asked. Now it made sense.

"A mixture," she answered. "Some of hers, some of mine. We couldn't share shoes, of course, but we shared accessories."

"I guess that's why you never had kids. I always wondered."

"Well, we thought about it." Her face betrayed no sadness. "Honestly, we did. We could have. But we were having so much fun, as friends. Why ruin it? Besides, she had Mabel." And she nonchalantly refilled her martini glass from the pitcher.

"Miss Mabel? The school secretary?" I couldn't believe what she was telling me!

"Welcome to Parkville, Dolly. Those late night soap operas have nothing on us."

"But I thought they were best friends!?" I said.

"Everyone did," she said. "Well, it depends on your definition of *friends*, I guess. Janey and Mabel were pretty steady, the whole time we were married. They were lucky. No one seemed to give two ladies a second glance, but anytime I had a 'special friend' I had to be more cautious. That's why I joined The Bears' Club. A bit more privacy."

Beret went on to explain that The Bears' Club had been a haven for closeted homosexuals, their close friends and straight allies for generations. Not everyone was gay, but it was a safe, accepting environment for men to enjoy the company of other men, without the interference of prying eyes, wives or pesky Southern morals. There once was a time when men were more homosocial, and it was just the norm. Sure, they had poker tournaments and fundraisers for community improvements, but what's wrong with the occasional variety or drag show? Nothing, as far as I could see. In fact, I was so proud of Parkville right now, I wanted to scream it from the rooftops. I just wished more people knew about it.

"That's the thing you have to promise me, Derek. This has to stay between you and me. No one else can know." She looked at me, very seriously. "Not a word to your mom, either. There are too many other lives and relationships at stake here, and we have to respect that. Some may choose to look the other way, but others in this town would not be so generous. This Supreme Grizzly is going to protect her den, and I expect you to back me up on that, okay?"

"You have my word." I held my hand to my heart. "Honor bright, snake bite."

"Good boy," and she turned to look in her vanity mirror, pulling tissues from the box. "Now, I need to touch up this makeup and go mingle. We have some new members upstairs, and I need to make a good impression. It can't hurt to have a few judges and lawyers on your side when you need 'em. Enjoy your night, doll. I love you."

"I love you too, Uncle Barry." Air kisses all around. "Oh. One last thing. That 'lady' on stage before you looked an awful lot like Mr. Bellman, the Parkville High School Principal. Was that just my imagination?"

"*Belle*? That bitch. Never do a duet with her. She'll upstage you every chance she gets. Trust me."

And with that, I popped up the staircase, out the back door and got into my car. I didn't think any movie at Tommy's could top the night I'd already had.

10

BOTTOM'S UP

I woke up Monday morning more excited for school than I had ever been in my entire life. I hadn't seen or heard from Luke since our good-bye hug on Friday night, and the mixture of emotions and hormones in my body were putting my head into overdrive. I am definitely guilty of overthinking. No news is good news, right?

Wille Nelson and I raced to the high school as fast as we could without getting caught in any of Parkville's (well known) local speed traps. All I could think of was Luke. What should I say to him? Am I wearing the right clothes? Will he smile when he sees me? Should I bring him a coffee? Maybe we can have lunch together? Maybe I could sit in on one of his classes during my planning period? I can't wait to see him, talk to him, hug him, smell him. I felt like a teenager again! David, who?

His car was already in the lot when I pulled in to park. My heart actually skipped a beat as I stepped out into the fresh autumnal air. Homecoming was just around the corner. Maybe we could chaperone the dance together? Ok, ok... don't get ahead of yourself, Derek. Let's start with something small, like going on a vacation together or choosing names for our imaginary kids. God, I'm crazy and I know it. I'm grinning from ear to ear.

I opened the door to the teachers' lounge and stepped in. There he was, sitting by the window with his nose buried in the sports section of *The Parkville Post*, Tennessee Volunteers baseball cap tipped back high on his forehead.

"Luke! Good morning. Coffee? I picked up two." I thrust a green paper cup towards him. "I picked up a latte and a regular. Wasn't sure which you preferred."

"No, thanks." He didn't even look up from his paper.

"It's no problem at all," I said. Why won't he look at me? "I just figured you might want a good coffee. Better than that new machine we have, don't you think?"

No answer.

"So, how was the rest of your weekend?" I asked. My heart started pounding. I was sinking, and I could feel it. "I guess you got home all right Friday night?"

"All good" he said, as monotonously as he could manage. He turned the page of the newspaper and kept reading.

Did I go too far? Did I say too much? I started to panic. When I start to panic, I start to sweat. And when I start to sweat, my mind starts racing, and any minute now my mouth was going to go places it clearly should not, given the situation at hand. Thankfully, I heard a voice of reason behind me.

"I'll take that coffee," said Bammy, from the doorway. "How sweet of you. Thanks, Derek." I turned to look at her and she gave me that *you get over here now* look that mothers so often give to their wayward children. I clenched my jaw, gritted my teeth and marched towards the door.

"Yeah. Sure," I said. "No problem. See you 'round." I dropped the cup in Bammy's hand and pushed past her rudely into the hall.

"Derek. *Derek!*" she whisper-screamed, chasing after me down the hallway in her heels. "What was that all about? What happened on Friday after we left? What are you doing? What are you thinking? He's *straight*. You *know* that. Derek!"

"Leave me alone, Bammy. I don't wanna talk about it." I picked up the pace and headed across the courtyard towards my first class. Obviously, Luke was choosing to ignore Friday night. He's all hugs and high fives when it's the two of us, but in school he's back to his old persona. Self-loathing asshole. All right, Luke, so this is the game we're playing, is it?

Well, I'm not interested.

■ ■ ■

I made up my mind that it was all in my mind.

I imagined it. I created it. I needed something romantic and hopeful and exciting after running away from David and my New York life, and Luke Walcott was just the ticket. He was perfect, in fact: yet another hot, athletic, unattainable straight boy for this lonely hopeless romantic to pine after. I always said I suffered from congenital sadness, but this time, I wasn't going to let "another one who got away" break me down. I'm better than that now. At least, I hope I am.

A week had passed since "The Showdown at the Coffee Corral," as Bammy called it. I don't know what I was thinking. Well, I do, but I didn't want to admit it to my friends, let alone to myself. I had fallen for the wrong guy, and even worse, I fell fast and hard after a single late-night hug. One hug! Was I that desperate for love?

Bammy and Kit talked me off the ledge and I regained my sanity fairly quickly. Luke and I didn't speak of "the incident," as I'm sure it was nothing to him. We said our casual helloes as we passed in the hallway, but we didn't go much further than that.

The weekend came faster than expected, and we headed on down to The Firelight, as we did every Friday night. The Scooby Gang staked out our usual booth, but Luke was nowhere in sight.

"Will you stop looking at the door?" Bammy said as she threw me a meaningful look over her Jack and Diet Coke. "He's not coming. And even if he did, it wouldn't be for you. So stop, okay? You're here with us."

She was right. I was obsessing while pretending that I wasn't obsessing. Stalking him was just around the corner, but I was trying to keep that side of myself at bay.

"Whatever," I said. "He's a douchebag. No, actually he wishes he were a douchebag. He's actually just unimportant. That's worse." I wasn't even convincing myself.

"He's not a douchebag, Derek," said Bammy. "He's actually a pretty good guy. He's just not the 'good guy' for you. One hug doesn't mean he's a closet case, you know? Not every handsome guy is gay, even though I know you wish that were the case."

"It has been my experience that men who feel the need to say they are 'good guys' are generally trying to convince themselves," Kit said. She had known her fair share of douchebags masquerading as improved souls. "But that doesn't matter, any way," she added. "You want to hate him. I get that."

"I just feel like I want to run away, again," I said. "Even though I just did that, coming here. Today I daydreamed that I was a French teacher in some military training facility. Then I realized it was all the men in uniforms that I found most appealing." I sighed. "Something is very wrong with me."

Kit looked at me and smiled a knowing half smile. "Derek, there's nothing wrong with you. You're just going to have to learn to deal with all the shit that doesn't magically fall into place. You have always believed that the universe owes you. You want to run away when things get tough. *We. All. Do.* That's normal. But you also want to hate everyone, and you expect all of us to love you while you're doing it. Not everyone will adore you, my friend. Just the special ones. Like us." And she winked at me.

Kit was right with her tough love. I wallow in self-pity, throw my accusations and lash out left and right, all the while protecting myself with a mask of vicious laughter. It's either that or cry? It had to stop. I moved back home to find myself again, and getting hung up on a straight guy and feeling sorry for myself wasn't part of the action plan. I needed to remember that it's more important to take care of myself, first. The rest will follow.

"Man, you just need to get laid," Tommy said and put his beer up to his lips. He took a big gulp, and then set it down with a wide grin. "You know I'm right. That's just tension speaking, and it's the kind of tension you can take care of pretty easily. Especially a gay guy. Hell, isn't there an app for that?"

"Fuck you," I said. "And I mean that with love, my friend."

The girls giggled, then moved in closer as I pulled my phone out of my pocket. Tommy was right. Again. One easy search for mobile phone apps and found my prize: Huntr, for gay men on the hunt. I downloaded it and made a quick profile, not adding anything that could be tied back to me, Derek. I called myself "Duke," as an homage to Derek and Luke. Thankfully, the girls didn't make the connection.

"*Ooooh*, very regal sounding!" said Kit.

I chose a photo that Bammy took of me down by the lake as my profile picture. Shirt off, legs hanging down off the dock into the water. I have my back to the camera and a baseball cap on. Even I think I look hot in this one.

"Now what?" said Bammy. "How does this Huntr thing work?"

"Well, you make a profile," I explained. "You say what you're looking for, then you just kind of wait. It's all based on GPS, so you can see when there are other guys on the app who are near you. Like this one, for example." I pointed out a picture of a really young blond twink with a cute smile. "He's less than a mile from us right now, and he's looking for some NSA fun." " 'NSA' means 'No Strings Attached,' Bammy," said Kit. "Men are so driven by hormones." They both laughed.

"So go for it!" said Bammy.

"Bammy, he's nineteen," I laughed. "He's practically one of our students. I'll pass. There must be something more my type around here. Well, hello Dolly!" Had I been hanging around Beret too much?

Someone who went by the handle "Cowboy" had posted a picture of his chest, and it was mighty fine: mid 30s, dark blond, no shaving, just my type. And only a few miles away.

"Here we go. I'll take 'Hot Pecs' for a thousand, Alex!" I sent a quick *hey, how's it going?* and he offered the same. He seemed cool and we started chatting. I didn't want to chat too much, and thankfully he didn't either. We both understood that this wasn't the kind of app for romance and a marriage proposal.

"Shit." I froze. "He wants to meet. What do I do?"

"DO IT!" the girls screamed, in unison. Tommy just laughed and took another drink.

"Okay. Here goes." I replied and hit send, without over analyzing for the first time in my life. "Shit. He answered. It's on. We're meeting in an hour at that gay bar out east, past the old bowling alley."

"That was so easy," said Bammy. "Why can't straight people just hook up like this?"

I paused. Lightbulb. "Oh, fuck. We never traded face pics."

I just asked a torso out for a drink.

■ ■ ■

Bottoms Up was located a few miles east of downtown Parkville in a derelict part of town. Just your average gay Southern white boy dive bar, it was known for its cheap drinks and even cheaper clientele. I'd only been there a few times in college when they had dollar nights, and back then we were pretty scared for our lives, but the super low prices helped to calm our fears. Did I mention how cheap the drinks were?

I parked Willie next to an old hearse that looked like it was straight from the set of *Six Feet Under*, and walked in the door. The jukebox here was nowhere near as good as The Firelight, and some shitty hybrid hip-hop pop crap was blaring through the speakers. "Cowboy" had informed me he would be wearing an orange and white baseball cap, but I didn't see him yet.

I figured I might as well get a drink while I waited, so I walked up to the bar. "Jack and Coke, please," I ordered.

"Just one?" the bartender asked. He was wearing blue jeans and a leather vest with no shirt and had a wad of chewing tobacco in his mouth. He looked down his nose at me with his one good eye.

"Yeah," I said. "I'm waiting for my friend."

"Y'all want a pitcher?" he said. "Eight dollars."

God bless you, Bottoms Up. I gave him a ten and took my pitcher of Jack and Coke and two glasses back towards one of the smaller tables near the pinball machines. I pulled out my phone and started up Huntr again. I took another look at "Cowboy," and he did, indeed, have a beautiful torso. But what about the rest of him? Unfortunately he was offline, and since we were both so averse to chatting, we hadn't traded any other information.

I poured a drink from the pitcher and took a look around. The vinyl seat beneath me was held together by duct tape, and the entrance to the bathroom was of the swinging half-door variety. I felt dirty just being here.

What *was* I doing here? Two months ago I was planning my wedding in Central Park to a man I thought I wanted to spend the rest of my life with. Then I played Runaway Bride and the next thing I know I'm on a plane to Tennessee. Now my uncle is a drag queen, I'm in love with a straight guy, and I'm afraid I'll catch something on the wrong side of town.

Wait. What did I just say? I'm in *love*? Oh, Derek, this is just sad. You don't want to be here. Tommy was right, I do need to get laid, but "Cowboy" isn't the answer. I deserve more than a torso.

I placed my drink on the table, stood up and headed towards the exit.

A group of twentysomethings auditioning for roles in a redneck update of *Cruising* hollered after me. "Hey, you done with that pitcher?" they asked.

"Yep," I said as I passed their table.

"Can we have it?" they asked.

"Knock yourselves out." And I walked out the door.

11

FIX UP, CLEAN UP

It's Monday again, but I'm not as crazy as last week, thankfully. I do not look for his car today as I pull into the lot. I do not run to the teachers' lounge like a puppy with my tongue falling out and my tail wagging behind me. I do not bring extra coffee and extra cheer for the man I am falling for, because it's more than apparent that he is not falling for me, as I had hoped and prayed and, obviously, imagined. It's a crazy man's dream that is slowly dying as I get my life back in order again.

We have a staff meeting in the morning. Bammy has an announcement to make, so I take my seat towards the back on a metal folding chair. Luke is somewhere in here. I guess. I don't know. I'm not looking.

"Homecoming is one of the most important weeks here at the school," she began, "and I'm sure I don't need to enumerate why. Alumni come from all over the state to reminisce about their days here in Parkville, and we want to make sure that we put on the best face possible. Coach Walcott is getting our team in shape for one heck of a football game, isn't that right, Luke?"

"Y'all know it!" he said. I could feel him standing somewhere behind me but I don't look. Remember, Derek. Don't look.

"Now," she continued, "just because we're not all playing in the big game doesn't mean we can't contribute. Y'all are aware that the school has seen its fair share of budget cuts, and there's a lot around here that could do with a little sprucing up. That's why we've asked all y'all to help us out this upcoming Saturday morning. We're going to split up into teams and do our best to make our school something to be proud of. Now let's hear some of that Commodore spirit!"

Woo hoo. Sorry, Bammy. That's the best I can do for you right now.

The week rolled by without incident and suddenly it was Friday. I bowed out of our regular Firelight gig. I just didn't have the energy. Mom made chicken and dumplings, green beans and deviled eggs, and then she and Uncle Barry and I crashed in the living room in our carb-induced haze to watch *Auntie Mame* on the DVD player. Barry and I have practically all the lines memorized, and we took turns one-upping each other with quotes. Seriously Mom, if we hit you over the head with this stuff, you may just have to comment on Barry's sexuality one day.

I woke up feeling fresh and headed on over to the school Saturday morning to help with "Fix Up, Clean Up." It felt good to get out of bed early without a hangover. Maybe I should consider skipping Friday nights more often? My liver would certainly appreciate the kindness.

There was a card table set up in the main hall with coffee and fresh baked doughnuts. They were still warm, straight from the bakery. They melted like little sugar pillows in my mouth as I greedily consumed one, two, three. Damn. So much for my healthy New York lifestyle.

"I'd like to thank y'all again for coming out here on a Saturday morning," Bammy started. "We've split everyone into groups with specific areas to tackle. Just find your name up here on these lists. To be fair, they're alphabetical, so we didn't play any favorites with the tasks. We'll work until noon, and then we have lunch provided by the Marching Band moms."

Alphabetical? Luke *Walcott*. Derek *Walter*. SHIT. Fuck you and your "fairness," Bammy. Did you even consider your bestie?

I looked up at the lists posted on the bulletin board and I'm part of the outside crew, helping to pick up any trash in the parking lot, pull weeds, wash exterior windows, that kind of thing.

"Looks like we're on the same chain gang," Luke said, over my shoulder.

"And here I am without my orange jumpsuit," I said.

He let out a small laugh. That was all I needed, and suddenly I was googley-eyed, all over again. I'm hopeless. I really am.

"Tired of avoiding me?" I said. "The freeze out wasn't so fun, you know."

"Freeze out?" he asked.

"Well, yeah. You were pretty quiet this week."

"Derek, you read way too much into things. Anybody ever told you that?"

"Just my whole life," I said, and cocked my head to one side.

"Well, maybe you should listen, then. And remember, not everything's about you." And with that he turned and walked towards the door.

I stood there, not sure what to think. Or overthink. Or over analyze. Or... anything. I was frozen. Do I like him? Do I not like him? Are we friends? Or more? What is real, and what am I imagining? Man, it sucks being a thirteen-year-old girl.

Luke's voice roused me from my thoughts. "*Yo.* Dreamer. You coming, or what? We got work to do."

"Uh... yep. Chain gang. Let's do it." And I followed.

We spent the morning clearing cans and errant cigarette butts from the parking lot and grounds before moving on to window duty. Even though it was officially autumn, it was still warm in the South, and it wasn't long before the sun came out in full force and Luke shed his jacket. I couldn't help but stare at this man in his white V-neck t-shirt, tight blue jeans and work boots as he hauled buckets of warm soapy water and towels. His biceps and pecs strained the tight confines of the white cotton tee, and soon the splashing water made the material rather see-through.

"Hey. Stop drooling and get back to work." Bammy laughed as she bumped up beside me.

"Shit! Sorry. Is it that obvious?" I asked, embarrassed.

"You look like a Wall Street banker at an all-you-can-eat stripper buffet," she said laughing.

"*Ack*. Thanks for that image. Seriously. I don't mean to sexualize him, but DAMN. Look at him!"

"Why do you think I alphabetized, silly?" She winked at me, and then moved on to check the progress of the next team.

All right, Bammy. You win this one. I was clearly wrong to be pissed at you.

I took another glance at Luke, and he was up on his ladder, reaching up high to get the top of the window frame. The bottom of his t-shirt had lifted up to expose his taught stomach, covered in a fine layer of dark blond scruff. My hand was holding the sponge to the window, but I'm sure it wasn't moving. There were streams of water cascading down the glass, but I was completely frozen, staring at the man of my dreams just a few feet from me. If I didn't know better, he was exaggerating his stretching and bending and reaching, just to give me the show of a lifetime.

My eyes slowly wandered from his stomach up to his chest, then to his face. He turned his head as if in slow motion, smiled, and paused what he was doing... and winked at me. Busted.

I can't. I seriously can't. Dear Lord, if I die right now, it will be enough.

12

AT THE LAKE

We went our separate ways after "Fix Up, Clean Up." Bammy wanted all the gossip, but my head was spinning. Truthfully, she was pissing me off a little. She can't be upset with me for chasing after a straight guy, then move all the chess pieces around so that I have no other choice but to chase a straight guy.

I woke up Sunday morning feeling as confused as ever. It's amazing what you can convince yourself of if you try hard enough. There was no denying that Luke and I had some sort of connection. Was it as simple as a blossoming friendship, or as wickedly illicit as a same sex attraction? To put it plainly, Luke was never going to ride on a Gay Pride float, but was he the kind of Southern gentleman who could find what he needed at The Bears' Club? Stranger things have happened.

I pulled myself out of bed and picked up my running clothes from the chair. If I didn't have a relationship, at least

I had running, again. I'd kept true to my promise of keeping it up, and I was now addicted to the high. Besides, all these carbs were killing me. How was I not enormous as a kid? Oh, that's right. All my multiple social anxieties just worried the pounds off.

There was a slight fog this morning as I drove Willie out to the park at the lake. Parkville Community Park was located just a short drive from Mom's house, and as kids we spent hours there playing on the swing sets and swimming in the large public pool. As teenagers, the park was where we drank our wine coolers and planned our escapes from this place. Funny. I escaped, then came right back. The cyclical nature of life, I suppose.

Since I moved away, the town had spent a lot of money on the park, installing new benches, upgrading the pool facilities and creating a clubhouse. They even set up a dedicated running path that circled the lake. I pulled the car off the main street into the upper parking lot at the top of the hill, where the running path started. There weren't too many spots there, as the main lot was over by the clubhouse, on the other side of the park. Sure enough, the small lot was full. Well, not really. There was a beat up old Ford pick up truck with a gun rack and an NRA bumper sticker that had parked over a painted line, taking up two spots. It was just that kind of day where the smallest thing was about to set me off. I maneuvered my car back around and parked down by the main street in the lower lot, then reached for a Chinese takeout menu from the floorboard of the car to use as scrap paper. I scrawled my angry message and then walked back up the hill and placed my handwritten note under the pick up's windshield wipers. It said ASSHOLE in large, black capital letters. I knew my note wouldn't have any effect, but it sure made me feel better.

I popped my headphones in, started my running app and a Madonna play-list, and took off. The first 5 minutes I felt like crap, but as I rounded the bend I started to feel the proverbial "wind beneath my wings." That elusive runner's high was about to be mine. I was completely in the zone. No David, no New York. No school, no Scooby Gang. No Luke, no romance.

I was keeping a great pace, when suddenly I felt the runner behind me shoot past me, turn, and wink. You guessed it. Luke Walcott. Damn it, Luke, this is one game I'm not going to let you win.

I pulled the headphones from my ears and used every trick I knew. Breathing in through my nose, out with my mouth, lifting my legs high and really engaging my thighs. Seeing him just within reach was pissing me off, but it was good. I'm competitive as hell, and I pushed faster, harder and stronger, until I was able to catch up to him. He flashed that perfect smile at me and kept pushing on, just as hard. We raced to the top of the hill, towards the home stretch. My legs were aching, my heart was pounding out of my chest, and I was gasping for air as we rounded the last corner and began our descent towards the lot, neck and neck. The rest of the path was downhill towards the parking lot, and I was going to try my damnedest to win.

"First. One. To. The. Oak. Wins," I managed to gasp out, with my last remaining breath.

"You're. On. Buddy!" he replied. And with that, we pushed forward. I was afraid to look next to me, but all I knew was that he wasn't in front of me. Was I actually winning? My momentum was propelling me forward so hard that I overshot the tree, and then collapsed on my back onto the green grass, gasping for air.

Luke came crashing down next to me, his chest heaving up and down, as we both stared up into the sky. You know that moment where something happens, but you're not sure how or why it started? Well, this was one of those moments. He started laughing, then I started laughing, and before you know it, we were rolling on the grass, cracking up.

He flipped over onto his stomach and said, "Damn, buddy. You can run!"

"I'm like a greyhound," I said. "I just keep my eye on the prize."

"Did you run in high school?" he asked. "I'm sure I would have remembered if you were on the track team."

"*Nah*. Didn't pick it up until I moved to New York. Central Park is a pretty good motivator. That and all the hot guys in shorts." I turned to him to gauge his reaction.

He looked down, a small grin forming on his face. Those dimples. "Well, whatever your motivation is, you're good. Better than me, I'd say."

"Thanks. That means a lot coming from you, Mr. Star Athlete."

"Well, I do have a few pounds on you," he said.

"Yeah, all muscle." Was I flirting? Oh, my god. I'm flirting.

"Take the compliment, man," he said. "You're an athlete, too. You just proved it."

I was on my back, one arm crooked under my head, the other on my chest. He was leaning on his side, one arm holding his head up, his eyes looking directly into mine. Sweat dripping down his forehead, he had never looked sexier. The past few weeks felt like such a dream to me, but what was the end goal? Another crush on a straight guy? No. This was something more. I felt it. I knew it.

Fuck it. Now or never. My heart felt like it was going to pound out of my chest as I leaned up slowly... and kissed him softly, once, on the lips. He didn't kiss back, but he didn't push me away, either. I pulled back, my heart pounding.

"Derek, I..." he started to speak, but stopped and just looked at me, with an air of sadness in his eyes.

"I'm sorry. I just. I don't know," I sputtered. "I've just wanted to, and I thought, well... I just did it. I'm sorry. God. I'm really sorry. I should go." I sat up in the grass quickly, ready to act on the urge to run away.

"No. Hey. Don't freak out. It's cool," he said, reaching out to place his hand on my arm, keeping me there. "If I were to be honest with you, I'd say... I'm glad you did it. I mean, I never would have. You kept your eye on the prize, right?"

"Wait. What?" Did I hear that right?

"I'm glad you did it," he said, quietly. "Made the first move. I was too chicken, Derek."

I stared at him, dumbfounded. I wasn't crazy! It wasn't all in my mind!

"Wait. What?!"

"You said that already." And he laughed, reached up with his hand and placed it on the back of my neck, and pulled me into him. The second kiss was soft and gentle, but the fireworks in my head were anything but.

We pulled apart, slowly, and I couldn't help but stare into his eyes as he looked into mine. "Holy shit," I whispered. "Luke *Fucking* Walcott just kissed me."

"I'd like to do more than kiss you, but we're kind of hiding behind a tree in a public park, and I'm about to freak the fuck out," he said. He was serious. I could see the mix of fear and lust in his eyes, and I remembered that emotion all too well. I could taste his sweat on my lips, and I wanted more, but I knew he was right. We needed to hightail it out of there.

"Yeah, sure, I get that. Let's get out of here," I said. We got up off the grass and walked slowly towards the parking lot. He kept his eyes towards the ground, but I could feel myself grinning for every gay boy on the planet who pined after that elusive man they always dreamed of but thought they could never get.

"So… you wanna hang out?" I asked. I hoped. "Do something? Move in together? Would you prefer a spring or fall wedding?" I didn't want this moment to end.

He laughed at my attempt at humor. "Slow down there, buddy. This is all kinda new to me, remember? No marriage proposals yet, okay?"

"Deal."

"I was thinking we start with something small. How about dinner this week?" he said. "I know a quiet place we can go, and the chef's pretty good. My place."

"Sounds great," I said. "I'm looking forward to it."

"Listen, I hope you understand. I don't think I can go *out* yet. Dinner at my place is a good start, but can we take it from there? And sorry, but I have to be 'that guy.' Can you keep Bammy out of this? I'm not a greyhound like you. I need to take this one pretty slow. Cool?" He looked over at me, his jaw muscles clenching and unclenching. I remember that fear of the unknown, and of course I had to respect his wishes.

"Absolutely. No Bammy," I said.

"What's this?" he said, as he pulled the note from the windshield of the pick up truck.

"Are you driving this?" I said. "But you have a Jeep?"

"It's in the shop. Scooter is replacing the alternator. This is my father's truck. What the fuck? Someone left a note that says ASSHOLE."

"Really? Huh. I wonder why?" Oh, shit. Oh, shit, Derek. Are you really going to screw this up before it ever begins?

"Some psycho wrote this rambling note that says I parked over the line. What a jerk! I had to. When I pulled in, the guy next to me was over the line, and I had no choice. It was the last spot," he explained.

"Oh, wow. Yeah, I get that. *Huh*. Wonder who could have left that note? What a jerk," I said, in what felt like my most unconvincing voice.

"Whatever. I'm not going to let some douche ruin my day. Not when I feel as good as I do right now." With that, he winked at me, opened the door to his borrowed car and hopped in. "Catch you soon, buddy. And uh, thanks." And with that, he was off.

I watched his car slowly drive away and my knees began to give out underneath me. I couldn't believe that all just happened. Am I breathing? He just kissed me and asked me out on a date. Luke just kissed ME. I floated down the hill on my wobbly legs and climbed into Willie.

Every fiber of my being was shaking with the full force of my emotions. I was a volcano about to erupt! And I promised Luke I would not tell Bammy anything.

But I didn't say a word about Kit...

■ ■ ■

I raced home from the park, pulled into our driveway and stepped into the living room. Uncle Barry was watching *Dancing With The Stars* while perched in his easy chair with his feet up on an overstuffed ottoman and a bowl of popcorn in his lap. Mom was in the kitchen checking on something in the oven.

"Hey guys, what's up?" I said. I was smiling. A lot. Perhaps too much?

"Well, someone's all a sparkle," Barry said, one eyebrow raised, hand reaching for his cocktail.

"Hi, sweetie," said Mom. "I wasn't sure if you were here for dinner tonight. I have enchiladas in the oven. Want to help me with the salad?"

"Cool. Do I have time for a quick shower? I'm heading out after dinner to meet Kit," I said.

"Sounds good. Be quick though, will ya? The enchiladas are basically ready." Mom liked us all to eat together, like a family. I think it was the one good constant in her life. She wasn't fond of dinners in front of the television. She preferred to have us sit around the table so we could catch up on our day. It was nice, actually.

I ran up to my room, sat on the edge of my bed and let out a little happy scream. It was so hard to not let myself get carried away, but this feeling was too intense to ignore. I had been right. I was really right! But then again, so many of the "right" ones in the past turned out to be total emotional breakdowns. Breathe, Derek, breathe. Maybe I need to ignore this one just a bit? Take it easy, and by all means, do NOT pressure him.

I was in and out of the bathroom in ten minutes and then down to the kitchen counter to put the salad together. Uncle Barry was setting the table as mom placed the enchiladas in the center and I plated three quick side salads. Those days spent in restaurant service during college were proving a lot more useful than that chemistry class I hated so much.

"So, you seem to be in a super good mood. Is it the job? We've barely seen you around here, honey," said Mom.

"*Mmmm* these enchiladas smell good!" I said, heaping my plate with food and hoping to avoid the *why are you so damn happy?* question. Quick. Get them talking about something else. "Work's been great, actually. Kind of strange to be back in that building, of course, but I'm getting used to that. I think in some ways you always feel like a kid in school, no matter how old you get."

"Stay young as long as you can," said Barry. "Trust me. The alternative isn't all it's cracked up to be."

"How's Bammy?" asked Mom.

"Oh, she's awesome. It's so good having her there to help me out. And I'm catching up with Kit and Tommy a lot, too. I didn't realize how much I missed them. I mean, they were always on my mind in New York, but coming back, it's like I never left. It's just so easy to get back in stride with old friends, you know?"

"Have you made any new friends?" She paused. Here it comes. "Anyone special?"

"Um, yeah. Sure. A few." How does she know these things? I swear she has magical powers.

"Well, you've got quite a bounce in your step tonight, so I was just wondering." She looked at me with those *you-can't-fool-me* eyes and I just smirked.

"*Ooooh*, gossip? Do tell!" said Uncle Barry, dropping his fork and reaching for his glass of wine.

"Hey. Stop." I looked at them both. "I don't need you two ganging up on me. All in good time, my loves! All in good time."

"There's something you're not telling us. But as long as you're happy, that's all I care about, sweetie." And with that, Mom seemed to let it go.

"Oh, wow, wouldn't ya know?" I said, unconvincingly. "Look at the time. Gotta run. Kit is expecting me at her place. Thanks for the food, Mom!"

I walked my plate over to the sink, grabbed the keys, checked my look in the mirror and hit the road.

13

CHESTY CHEESE

Sunday night was the best night to hit the strip club, and Kit and I were on the guest list, thanks to Scooter's girlfriend, Tammy. It *is* good to have friends in low places, I guess.

Chesty Cheese was Parkville's premiere "Gentlemen's Club," but let's be honest; there weren't any gentlemen there. Chesty Cheese started out as a Chuck E. Cheese's franchise. Part pizza parlor, part kiddie arcade, this particular location took an economic dive in the early 90s with the advent of home gaming systems, and then the franchise owner passed away in a decidedly non-family way. He had a heart attack in the bed of his girlfriend, a local stripper named Peaches.

Peaches had a great sense of humor, obviously, and Chesty Cheese was born. It didn't matter if you were straight or gay, young or old, rich or poor, black or white, everyone was welcome at her club. There were no judgements and very few rules.

Fridays and Saturdays were full of out-of-towners looking for a thrill they couldn't find in their own Bible Belt town, so we locals preferred our own night for fun. Chesty's was our place to be on a Sunday night. Plus, they had really good pizza.

Kit was decked out in a tribute to Wynona Ryder, circa *Beetlejuice*, complete with midnight blue pillbox hat and black zig-zag tights. Very Parkville. Not. But that's why I adored her.

"Aren't you excited?" she asked. "We're gonna have *So. Much. Fun!*" Kit placed emphasis on Every. Single. Word. "I stopped by the bank and picked up a hundred in singles, so you get ready to party, Mr. New York. *Oooh!* There's a table upfront by the best pole. Let's grab it, quick!"

"I adore you," I said.

"I know." She marched straight ahead, full of purpose.

"The 'best' pole? You crack me up."

"Baby, it's like the movies," she explained. "You don't wanna sit too far towards the edges. It messes with your sight line."

"Wow. I get ya. Does Shawn know you have strip club attendance broken down to a science?" I said.

"Who do you think taught me?" She grinned and flagged down a cocktail waitress. "Hey, Charlotte! You look so good tonight. *Love* your hair! Two vodka martinis, please. And tell Bobby we want 'em very dry. You know the drill. Just tell him to open the bottle of Vermouth, think about pouring some in there, then change his mind. Three olives, no twist. And keep 'em coming." She turned back towards me with a smile. "It's a martini night, babe. We have to show these rednecks how to party in style."

"Here's to us!" I said.

"Now, Derek, I can see on your face that something's up. You can't hide anything from me! You are *way* too happy, and I love that. I totally do. But I don't want to see you crash. 'Cause I'm the one who's gonna have to pick up all the pieces. *Tell. Me. Everything.*"

But before we could get started, we heard the opening bars to "Stand By Your Man," by Miss Tammy Wynette. That could only mean one thing. Our very own Tammy was on her way to the stage! Her act was flawless, and she really got the crowd going. Twirls, batons and enough pole action to make even the toughest fireman blush, she finished with a full split downstage center in front of our little table, pasties twirling and hands extended to the heavens. I'm surprised she didn't figure out a way to incorporate sparklers, but maybe she was saving those for later?

"Hey, y'all! So glad you could make it," said Tammy as she climbed off the little stage. "Mind if I take a seat? These killer heels are killing me."

"Tammy, you were awesome! How the hell did you learn all that pole action?" I said. "I am so impressed."

"A gay guy complimenting me on my way with a pole?" Tammy laughed. "Well, that's the best compliment I've had in years. You can come by anytime, sugar!"

"Don't make me blush!" I said. "You know what I mean. I'm just impressed."

"Well, thank you," she gushed. "Listen, I'd love to catch up with y'all right now, but I need to get going while the going's hot. I'm still fresh on their minds, you know?"

There was a group of men starting to crowd in, hungry looks in their eyes and twenty-dollar bills at the ready.

"Jeez, Tammy, there's a line forming!" said Kit.

"You're kind of popular," I said.

"Yeah. I know a lot of guys. It's kind of like one of them clown cars. Don't tell Scooter too much, though. He loves me. He does. And he thinks it's awesome to show me off, but he'll get his knickers in a twist if he thinks I'm too popular. I'll catch y'all later. Momma's gotta work hard for the money." And she was off to the lap dances.

"She is a firestorm," I said. "I honestly don't remember her being that fun in high school."

"She kinda blossomed after her chest caught up and then surpassed the rest of us. Cheers to Tammy's tits!" With that, Kit raised her martini glass to mine.

"To Tammy's tits!" I laughed and took a sip of pure chilled vodka and three olives.

"Now, baby. Spill," said Kit. "What's up? Or rather... *who's* up? It's gotta be a guy. I've seen that face before. *I. Know. You. Well.*" She smiled, warily.

I sighed. Honestly, I was a bit nervous and a bit scared, all at once. I promised Luke I wouldn't say anything to Bammy, but now I was about to violate that trust on a technicality.

"Ok, here goes," I started. "But you have to promise me. Pinky swear. Honor bright, snake bite. What I'm about to tell you, you can not tell another living soul, okay?"

"Yes! Spill!"

"You have to swear." I looked at her with as much seriousness as I could muster.

"I swear! Honor bright, snake bite. You have my word. Jeez. The build up. This had *Better. Be. Good.*"

"Luke Walcott." Beat. "It's Luke Walcott," I said and stared at her, waiting for a reaction.

She looked at me with unblinking eyes for what seemed like 5 minutes, but in all honesty it was probably around fifteen seconds.

Finally, she spoke. "*Holy. Shit.*" She grabbed her drink and took an enormous gulp.

"Now that's the reaction I wanted!" I said, satisfied.

"Luke Walcott?!" she stammered. "But, baby, isn't he? I mean, *wasn't* he? Or is he *now?* I mean, I know you were crushing on him *hard* when you first came back, but that was over and done with in a heartbeat, right? You said he was straight. We established that. Didn't we? Jeez. So confused. Your team is just recruiting all the hotties."

"I know, right?" I gushed. "He's everything. Athletic, smart, funny, hot as hell. And that smile and those dimples. I feel like it can't be true. But it is. We kissed. Today. I kissed him, and not only did he *not* freak out, he invited me over for dinner this week."

"*Holy. Shit.* This just gets better." She took another large sip of her martini and looked at me wide eyed. "I'm shocked. But, honestly? Not that shocked. Look at you. *Look. At. You!* Who could resist?"

"Oh, stop!" I could feel my cheeks reddening. "Kit, I'm terrified. I can't fuck this up. He's a newbie. I don't think he's done anything with anyone. Any guy. You know what I mean. But you know how I get. Look at my past. I'm crazy. I start to plan the wedding on the first date, and on the second date I've named the kids. By the third date I'm trying to figure out where we should retire. I'm insane. You have to help me!"

"You have got to go slow, Derek," she cautioned. "You cannot freak this one out. Luke is a total keeper. Hell, half the town will want to *be* you and half the town will want to *kill* you. He's the real deal, the maximum prize. Oh, shit. I know so many girls who are gonna wanna go all Rambo on you!" She playfully high fived me and then started laughing, uncontrollably. *"Best. News. Ever!"*

"I promised him I wouldn't tell Bammy, so I kind of cheated by telling you. Please, please don't tell anyone. But you have to help me with this. If I freak out, I just need someone to calm me down, okay?"

"Well, like I said, in a way I kind of knew already. At least, I hoped it would work out for you. But I'm here for you, baby. You know it. Oh my gosh I'm so proud of you!" She was really smiling now. I felt so much better having opened up to her. "You already cracked the shell, but we need to make sure he thinks you are every bit as wonderful as we all know you are."

"How do we do that," I asked, "when I either project this strange animosity towards him or practically go weak in the knees every time I see him? There's way too much intense love/hate right now."

"Confidence, baby." She stared straight at me. *"Confidence. Is. Sexy.* You have to show Luke that you're the kind of guy that HE wants. Now let's get started on a plan. But first, Charlotte?!" She held her hand up and called for the waitress, again. "Honey, we're gonna need a new round of drinks. Derek and I have some work to do. Oh! And can we get two of those mini pizzas? The one with the capers and lamb sausage? Thanks, girl!"

Let the Love Games begin.

14

TABLE FOR TWO

Kit and I spent the better part of the night at Chesty Cheese planning every moment of my upcoming dinner with Luke. In between martinis, pizzas and a few flying pasties we decided what clothes I would wear, topics of conversation, compliments I should give and subjects I should avoid. We even scheduled and pre-wrote an "emergency text" from her that I could answer or ignore, depending on how the night went.

Monday's hangover was vicious, but worth every minute. I'm telling you, when you want to plan an invasion in style, you want Kit Lange on your side. Before the war has even begun she'll have your enemy cozying up to you trying to figure out a way to become besties.

I was straightening up my desk at the end of the workday when one of my students knocked on the door and wheeled in a large rolling rack of clothes. "Mr. Walter? You have a delivery from the Home Ec class? Costumes for the musical?" Why do kids nowadays end every sentence in a question mark?

"*Ooh*, yes. Put it in there," and I pointed to the wardrobe closet in the corner. "Thanks so much."

I had been drinking water all day, but my head was ignoring the relief and was still pounding. All I wanted was a good run after work, but I knew I would collapse in agony after just a few minutes, so I pulled out my phone to put together a new playlist for another less headache-y day.

"Hey, handsome. Whatcha doin'?"

I looked up to see Luke smiling at me from the door, standing there in his jeans and tight grey t-shirt. Just the man I always wanted, in the flesh.

"Not much," I smiled, playing it cool. "Just putting together a Madonna playlist for my next run. And that's not even the gayest thing I've said today, by the way. That was '*Ooh*, yes. Put it in there.'"

Crap. Kit warned me not to go "too gay," and here I am, cracking Madonna and sex jokes.

Thankfully, he just laughed a bit and looked at me with a resigned look. "Derek, you don't have to try so hard. I know you're a funny guy. I like that. That's part of the reason why I like you so much." He smiled. "So I was thinking about that date. See you Wednesday, 8 o'clock? I'll text you my address. Don't be late."

And with that, he turned and left, leaving me with my jaw slightly dropped, my eyes wide open, and my headache a thing of the past.

Luke "likes" me.

And I didn't even have to pass him a note to ask.

■ ■ ■

"Break a leg, Dolly."

Uncle Barry was in his lounge chair as I came down the stairs. I'd been in and out of the bathroom and bedroom countless times, adjusting, readjusting, and basically sweating the good scent off so much that I had to reapply it.

"That obvious?" I said.

"What's his name?" he asked, from his usual spot in the long chair.

"I can't divulge that information, Uncle Barry. You of all people should appreciate how much we value secrets in this town." I winked at him.

"*Touché*, nephew" he said, eyebrow arching as he placed his glass of wine down on the side table.

Luke grew up a bit further out west, where the barns and pastures gave way to golf courses and rambling McMansions. His parents, Red and Posy Walcott, were well known in the community, but I had actually forgotten that his mother had passed away, if I even knew that at all. Even so, his childhood experience was definitely more "have" than "have not." After attending our local state university on a football scholarship, which he didn't actually need, Luke stayed in town and became a coach and teacher, leaving his dreams of playing pro football behind. He was good on the gridiron, but not great enough. Those who can't do, teach, right? He now lived towards the university in an older part of town known for it's refurbished Victorian houses.

I loved it there, as most of the architectural gems of the college campus had been razed for parking garages years ago. I appreciated that he had an eye for something with character. And I had plenty of that.

I parked on the street in front and walked towards his front door with a bottle of wine in my hand, the dual glow of the moon and a streetlamp lighting my path. I stood at the door nervously for a second, gathered my thoughts and took a deep breath. Here we go, Derek. As RuPaul says, "Don't fuck it up."

I rang the doorbell, and waited. And waited. And waited. Thirty seconds passed and it felt like an eternity. I didn't hear any foots steps, no one calling out to "come on in." So I pressed it again, and again there was nothing. No Luke, no welcome, no hug. And my mind started reeling.

Oh, my god. This is a set up. This is a joke. What if this is a joke? What if this is an elaborate, years-in-the-making joke? Oh, my god, I need to get out of here. I need to run. I can't believe I fell for this. I can't, I just can't. I couldn't breathe.

I stepped backwards off the porch and started walking back towards my car… and stopped. Hold up, Derek. You're acting like a crazy man and you haven't even walked in the door yet. Get your head in the game and get back there. Are you a greyhound? Do you want the prize, or not? Of course you do. Stupid question. Back straight. Eyes forward. Now, GO.

I turned, stepped back up, and tried the door handle. It opened. "Hello? Luke, it's me," I called out.

"Hey, come on in!" he said, from inside the house. He walked towards the door, extended his hand and pulled me in, closing the door quickly after me. Kitchen towel over his shoulder, he looked every bit the chef in charge.

"Um, sorry, I rang the bell but there wasn't an answer."

"Oh, yeah. Sorry about that. The bell's broken," he explained. "I guess I should really fix that. But you're here now. Good." He smiled and placed his arm around me, with his hand at the small of my back. "Come on in. Dinner's almost ready."

Of course there was a good explanation! Broken doorbell. My god, I almost left! I almost didn't come in. Remember what Kit said, Derek. Confidence is sexy. Be confident, be yourself, but keep that drama to a minimum.

I followed him into the kitchen. He had set the table for two, and there was a large pot on the stove that smelled fantastic. He had a cutting board out ready to chop some vegetables.

"I hope you like chicken," he said. "We used to have Mexican food a lot when I was a kid. My parents weren't around all that much. Rosa did all the cooking and cleaning. She took care of my little sister, Lana and me. She practically raised us, more than either of my parents, actually. My mother had always been too busy with her shopping and my father was always at his club. And after Mother was gone, my father disappeared in his own way. Anyway, this isn't a therapy session." He stopped, embarrassed. "Sorry about that. I'm kinda nervous, actually. Am I babbling?"

"No, it's okay," I said. "I'm happy to hear your stories. I just want to get to know you better, you know?"

"Yeah, me too," he smiled. "Anyway, Rosa made amazing meals for us, and I guess I paid more attention than I realized. I'm pretty good at this stuff. Hand me that avocado?"

I jumped up and sat on the counter beside him. "Mind if I sit? I like it up here. I always sat on the counter as a kid when my mom was cooking," I said.

"Is your mom a good cook? What's she make?" he asked.

"A little of everything. You and I can have a cook-off some day, to compare," I said.

"You're on." He winked at me. I melted. "Grab those plates from the table, will ya? I hope you're hungry."

We put together our plates of soft shell tacos, fresh salsa and avocado and walked over to the table. He had set it so that I was at the end and he was on the side, to my right, rather than across from me. We put our plates down and started eating, and he wasn't lying, he had apparently learned a lot from Rosa. The food was fantastic. We refilled our glasses of wine a few times and talked a bit more about growing up in our small town, and compared his choice of staying and becoming a football coach to my choice of leaving.

"So, what do you do in your spare time," he said, "besides drinking at The Firelight and running around the lake?"

"My life isn't all drag shows and shopping, if that's what you're thinking," I said, sarcastically. "I hang with my friends, I read, I write, I watch the games."

"You watch sports?" he said.

"Luke, I grew up in the same town as you did, remember?" I said. "If we didn't pay attention to football, there was definitely something wrong with us. I'm a Vol fan, like you. I'm just a bit tired of always saying 'this is a rebuilding year,' as if that's an excuse for our shitty plays on the field."

"Holy shit!" he laughed. "Not only can you catch a football, but you can talk football!" He smiled.

"Sure can. And I even know what I'm talking about." I took another sip of wine and gazed at him over the rim of the glass. This was going well. Keep it together, Derek.

He grinned at me and paused. "Are you happy you came back?" he asked.

"At first, I wasn't sure I did the right thing," I admitted. "I have a tendency to run away. I ran away from here to New York, and then I ran away from New York to come back here. So at first, I was unsure. But I gotta tell you, right now it feels pretty damn good."

He smiled at me and took a sip from his wine glass. It felt as though his eyes were burning a hole in me, he was staring so intently. On Kit's advice, I had worn a blue and white checked button down, with the top two buttons unbuttoned, exposing just enough chest hair and a hint of my pectoral muscles. "Hey, you got 'em, why not flaunt 'em," Kit had said.

I decided to make a move. "See something you like?" I said, and popped open one more button. His eyes traveled down to my chest, and didn't stray. He just nodded, slowly, as if in a trance.

"I'm really attracted to dark haired... guys," he said, as if saying the words for the first time made them true, and he needed to remind himself that it was okay. The next thing I knew, he reached up with his left hand, placed it behind my neck, and pulled my mouth forcefully to his. This was no soft, light kiss in the park. This was it. This was everything. Passion, emotion, pounding hearts and groping hands. We stood up so fast we knocked the chairs down behind us. He grabbed me by the waist and lifted me up along the wall. I felt as though he was going to consume me, and I loved it. His skin smelled of campfire wood, just as I remembered from our first hug outside my house after that night at The Firelight. The scent fueled my passion, and every sense was awakened. He reached down and pulled open the few remaining buttons of my shirt, and looked up at me while kissing my chest.

He stopped. "You're vibrating," he said.

It was my phone. The "emergency call" from Kit. "Ignore it," I said.

"You sure?" he asked.

"Bedroom." I said. *"Bedroom. Now."*

Without hesitating, he pulled me by the hand and led the way.

■ ■ ■

I woke up the next morning and opened my eyes, but I didn't want to move. I was in his bed with his arms around me, and I could hear him breathing softly under me, my face on his chest. I strained my head to look up at him, sleeping peacefully. I didn't want to wake him just yet. I must have stared at him for ten full minutes. I wanted to remember this moment forever. Suddenly, the alarm went off and his eyes opened, looking straight at me.

"Morning, stranger," he said.

"Hey. I just woke up," I lied and let out a play yawn and stretch. "How'd you sleep?"

"Good. Nice." He pulled me up to him and gave me a morning peck on the lips. "Very nice, actually. Damn. We have to get going. It's a school day."

"Can't we call in sick?" I said.

"Not today, buddy. I have that big Homecoming game coming up, remember?"

"Who could forget," I said. "*Rah rah.*"

He playfully slapped me on the butt and said "Come on. It's time to hit the showers."

"Are you seriously trying to fulfill every one of my prepubescent fantasies in 24 hours?" I said.

"I'll do my best," he grinned. I was mesmerized, watching his perfect ass walk away from me out of the room. I lay there for a second on the bed to collect my thoughts as I heard the water turn on down the hall. Last night had been amazing. We had kissed and fooled around and crawled all over each other's bodies, but it didn't go as far as it could have, and I was fine with that. Like I told Kit, Luke was a newbie, and it was so beautiful to watch his eyes open wide like a kid's at Christmas as we explored this new territory together. We both have well-formed, dominant personalities so it will be interesting to see how this evolves, but just thinking about it made me "ready" all over again.

"You coming or not?" he cried out over the sound of the water.

I walked into the bathroom to see his silhouette through the shower curtain. Arms up above the showerhead, mouth open, letting the hot water run down the muscles of his body. I pulled the curtain aside and stepped in behind him, placed one hand on his ass and curled the other around his chest, kissing him softly on the neck. He moaned and turned, slowly, then kissed me with the same passion he had shown the night before, holding my head in his hands.

"There's no time to play," he grinned. "Let's get down to business." He reached for the bottle of liquid soap. "Stand back," he said. "We have a few more fantasies to fulfill." And with that he began to wash my body.

"You're pretty good at this," I said. "You sure you've never done this before?"

"Nope. Just thought about it. A lot," he said, as his hands glided over my skin. "You know what it's like around here. Just the thoughts can get you taken down."

We stepped from the tub and began to towel off. I followed him back into the bedroom to get dressed and realized my clothes were spread out on the hallway floor, from the kitchen to the bedroom. I picked up my underwear, jeans and shirt and began getting dressed while he picked out new clothes from his dresser.

"I can't find my socks," I said. "Where did you throw my socks?"

"Here, take a pair of mine." He tossed a pair into my open arms.

"But then I have to wash and return them," I said.

"That's cool. I'm kind of looking forward to having you back." He smiled.

He was perfect. Nothing could go wrong. Right?

15

HIGH TEA

The next few days were a rush of conflicting emotions. I thought of him constantly, but could hear Kit in the back of my mind telling me to calm down and take it easy. "Ignore him a little," she counseled. But it was hard. Well, everything was hard, literally, every time I thought of him. I was able to avoid a few awkward moments in school by hiding behind my desk or stepping into the teachers' restroom for some privacy, but it's like my body had a mind of its own. I was a teenager again, and even in the same school. These are the times that I wish I were a smoker, so I would have an excuse to go out and "get some fresh air."

Seeing him in the hallways was even more difficult. He'd smile with his eyes down, but just enough so that I could see it. Overall, we still acted like strangers, "frenemies," even. And I had to accept that, for now. But for how long?

From my own experience, I knew that coming out was a process, and if I, in any way, tried to influence his decisions or push him too hard, there was a greater chance that he would fall right back into that Locker Room closet, and not into my open arms in front of our friends and families. I needed him to feel comfortable with his choices, and he had to be the one to decide when, and who to tell.

In the mean time, I was satisfied with the occasional text message and the furtive glance. It had only been a few days since our dinner, but I was already thinking of when and how to see him again. We hadn't made any plans, but I was hoping for the weekend. It's so hard to be the pursuer when you know the one you are pursuing needs you to be patient.

I went for a run by the lake after work. I didn't tell Luke I was going, but I sent many a silent prayer to the heavens that he would magically show up and we could recreate our first kiss. I'm such a hopeless romantic. And an idiot. Of course he wasn't there, but I ran an extra lap just in case he showed up. By the time I got home I was a mess, my mind going in a million different directions, talking myself in and out of love countless times.

I pulled into the driveway just as Uncle Barry was walking out. He had his faux Louis Vuitton duffle bag slung over his shoulder. I bought it for him in Chinatown years ago, and it looked so worn in now that it almost seemed authentic.

"Hello, Dolly. Why the long face?" he asked.

"Ah, *blah*. You know. This and that, school," I said.

"And men?" he said. "Or shall we say, one particular man?"

I glowered at him and nodded. Like Mom, I believe that Uncle Barry had a few magical powers of his own. He always knew things. That and the fact that I carry my heart on my sleeve. Everyone says my face is an obvious roadmap of my emotions.

"Listen, I have to run," he said. "I'm rehearsing a new number. But you, nephew, are coming by to see me tonight. Just come by the stage door again. I'll tell Scotty to expect you in about an hour. Now go shower and get a move on. It's high time you and I sat down for High Tea." He gave me a quick peck on the cheek and he was off.

High Tea? I love how my Uncle Barry was suddenly my gay Uncle Barry, like the fairy godmother from Fire Island Pines I always wanted and needed. I walked inside and took a shower, the whole time thinking of Luke and our situation. Maybe a chat with Barry would help, after all?

I parked in the lot at The Bears' Club and walked around back to the same red lacquered door I had entered when I first discovered Barry was Beret. Scotty was standing at the exit and he waved me in with a hushed *shhhh* finger over his lips. Walking over to the stage curtain, I could hear Adele's "Turning Tables" coming from the sound system. Beret was on stage and the house was empty, but she was giving it her all, mournfully lip syncing the words to a lost lover.

A tear fell from her eye as she finished the song, and my heart fell. I know Aunt Janey had been in love with Miss Mabel, the school secretary, but had Barry ever loved… and lost? Could I ever understand the battles, internal and real, that Barry's generation had fought so that men like me could fall in love with a high school football coach?

"*Bravo!*" I clapped and broke the silence. Beret turned to look and me, a demure smile spreading across her face.

"Oh, you," she said from the stage, and wiped away a tear. "You have to clap. You're family." She walked towards me, with purpose. "Scotty? I'm feeling a Pimm's Cup right about now. Can you bring a pitcher down to my dressing room? Thanks, Dolly."

"Sure thing, Beret" said Scotty, as he obediently dropped his clipboard on the table and headed to the bar. I followed my uncle downstairs to her private room and she sat once again in front of her mirrored vanity.

"Ok, Derek," she said, looking at me squarely. "Let's go. What's his name, and do I have to break any legs?"

"No, not at all," I said, smiling. I liked how she was protecting me. "It's nothing like that. It's going pretty well, actually. It's just that, well, he's closeted, and I don't know if that's something I want. I really like him, though. I think I may even love him. I mean, it's early, but I can feel that tug on my heart. I miss him when he's not there, and I think about him constantly. But I want to hold his hand, you know? I want to kiss him in a bar. I want everyone to know that he's mine, that we are a 'we,' that he's... he's gay."

Beret sighed, just as Scotty opened the door to deliver our cocktails. "Thanks, Scotty. A little family talk here. Take a break and I'll be up as soon as I can."

"Sure thing, Beret," said Scotty. "Take your time. You are the star, after all."

"And don't forget it, bitch." Beret laughed as Scotty closed the door after himself, then returned to her "serious" face.

"Now, back to you, my sweet nephew. Here's what I have to say, and you may not like it."

I braced myself for the deluge. Uncle Barry was never one to hold back, and I expected Beret to be the same, with simply a different, glittery surface coat painted on.

"Here's what I think," she started. "I think you deserve all the happiness in the world. I love you, kid, and you know that. But you have to decide what level of happiness is acceptable for you. In my generation, we didn't have so many choices. You could remain in denial of your sexuality and fight against it, at all odds. You could lead a dual life, as your Aunt Janey and I did, which meant an existence of elaborate lies and cover-ups. The closeted life to which you refer. Or you could be an out and proud *nelly queen*, but those ladies didn't make it very far in this town. That meant moving on to a bigger, more accepting city, or ending up beaten on the streets somewhere, dripping in blood as you stumbled home in the dark. I've seen it all, honey, believe me. You kids nowadays don't understand how good you have it. You are so special. You have so many choices, so many options. There are gay role models on the television, there are out actors and singers, authors and athletes. You can be anything and anyone your heart desires. You have access to so much. Too much, maybe. So, for me, in my situation, I made a choice to remain closeted, and just be out to my closest friends, and the members of The Bears' Club, of course. There was someone, once. But it didn't work out. I felt it more than he did. He and I had to make a choice, and we chose our families, instead of each other. But that's my situation. I am not you, and you are not this man you have feelings for. All of our journeys, all of our details and reasons, all of our expectations of life are different. You have to make the best choice for you, my love, and if he comes along for the ride, then he'll be the luckiest guy I know. Because you deserve pure, real love, my boy. That much I know."

I didn't know what to say or how to respond. I knew she was right, and as the tears welled up in my eyes, she reached over and gave me a tight hug, patting me on the back.

"Now stop it. No more tears," she said. "This mascara isn't waterproof."

I laughed over her shoulder as the teardrops fell from my eyes. "Thank you, Barry. Beret. I love you so much. Now let go of me. Your fake tits are freaking me out."

"What?! These cost me a fortune," she shrieked. "Here, feel."

We laughed together and settled back into our seats.

"So, I hope that helped. Now, are you going to tell me? Who is this young man who has stolen your heart?" she asked.

"I promised I wouldn't say anything," I responded. "Kit pretty much guessed, and Bammy can't be too far behind her, so I guess it doesn't matter much, anymore. Not to you, at least." I paused as my heart pounded. "It's Luke Walcott. The football coach at the high school."

Beret grew silent, pursed her lips and looked at me.

"What?" I said. "Do you know him?"

"Oh no, dear. Not personally," she said. "I've seen him though. Very handsome. Very handsome, indeed."

She raised an eyebrow and her glass and took another sip.

16

TOMMY TIME

On Sunday afternoon I gave Tommy a call.

"Hey," I said, as he answered the phone. "You up for lunch? How about sushi? I need some Tommy Time."

"Yeah man, sounds good," he said. "Swing by my place and we can walk to Saul's, downtown. Meredith is just headed out to meet her mom. Like, thirty, forty minutes?"

"Perfect," I said. "See you, soon," and I hung up. I couldn't really talk to Bammy, and I'd already been counseled with Kit's plan of action, but the truth of the matter was, I just needed some drama free time with my best guy friend. And, more importantly, I didn't want to talk about me. David sucked all the oxygen out of my life sometimes, but now I felt like I was becoming too much the center of attention, and I could really use a calm day where I could fade into the background a bit.

Tommy lived downtown in a renovated loft apartment. I parked Willie out front and went up to his place, letting myself in after a quick knock on the door. From the looks of the living room, it seemed like Meredith had pretty much moved in. I was happy for him. Tommy deserved only the best, and we all liked her a lot.

"Hey, man. How's it going?" he asked. He was sitting on the couch putting on his shoes. The cat was stretching languidly at his feet, and the coffee table was covered in leftovers from the night before: popcorn, peanut butter pretzels and two bourbon tumblers with the glassy sheen of melted ice.

"All good. Movie night?" I asked, looking down at the empty glasses.

"Yeah, we took it easy last night," he said. "Netflix. Meredith is having some kind of family brunch today, so she didn't want to show up with too big of a hangover."

"You didn't want to go?" I asked.

"Yeah, well, it's kinda early for family stuff," he said. "Besides, if I meet her family, then she'll want to meet mine, and I'm trying to avoid that as long as possible. The Pruitts aren't exactly the winners of the 'All American Family' award."

We both smiled. "Understood," I said.

"Saul's?" he asked.

I nodded. "Let's go!"

Saul's Sushi was another fine example of the local tradition of wearing our quirkiness with pride. Saul and his wife Rachel owned the only authentic Jewish deli in town, but as the downtown business district slowly died, his customers moved farther and farther west. As a result, Saul saw his business take a sharp downward trend. A Russian Jew, Saul and his family had arrived in Brooklyn in the early 1940s. He married Rachel and moved to the South to avoid the cold winters, while his relatives relocated west to Los Angeles, seeking year round sun and dreams of the movie business. One summer in the mid 80s when Saul and Rachel were considering shuttering the deli due to too many struggling years, they paid a visit to see their family in Los Angeles, and they were amazed to find teenagers at the local shopping malls eating sushi. Raw fish! Saul's Jewish Deli wasn't doing so well, so he bet the bank on a conversion he truly believed in, and Saul's Sushi was born. The interior was still Brighton Beach, but the menu was Jewish Japanese.

"How y'all doing today?" the hostess asked. "Two for brunch?"

We nodded and she sat us at a two top along the sidewall. "Can I get y'all some drinks before you order?" she asked.

"Yes, please," I said. "I'll have one of those Japanese beers."

"Make that two," Tommy added, nodding.

"I'll be right out with those," she said. "Here's a look at today's specials."

We took a look at the menu and when she came back we ordered an assortment of Saul's specialties; matzah ball egg drop soup, lox rolls and the potato pancake maki.

"Let's get some sake?" I asked. "If we're gonna day drink, we may as well do it right. Excuse me?" I flagged down the waitress. "Can we get a bottle of that unfiltered sake? The one that tastes like green apple. Thanks." I could never remember the name.

"So," Tommy started. "What's up? Wanna tell me about this mystery guy you're seeing?"

"Not just yet," I said. "Can we just talk about you? I feel a bit like Hurricane Derek right now. All the news, all the time, 24/7."

"Well, what do you expect, man?" he said. "You're kind of like that, sometimes. Kit and Bammy love being a part of The Derek Show." He took a sip of his beer.

"Yeah, I know," I said. "I'm kind of a big deal."

We laughed and clicked our bottles together. "Tell me about Meredith," I said.

"Man, she's awesome." Tommy smiled, and I could see that it was genuine. He had dated his fair share of crazies. I guess we all had. But it seemed that Tommy had finally found a girl who could balance her crazy between a bit of wild fun and a calm side.

"She's just cool," he said. "I feel comfortable with her, and I don't feel like I have to try extra hard to make her smile or make her happy. I don't have to think about it. We just kinda fit together well. There's no drama, no lies, no games. She just tells it like it is, and I appreciate that."

"I'm so happy for you, man," I said. "You really deserve it."

"Yeah, well you do too, you know." He looked at me with a half smile and said "I know the shit you've gone through, too, Derek. I love ya man and I just want you to be happy."

"I'm good," I said. "He's a lot different from David, that's for sure. But it's not as easy as you and Meredith."

"How so?" he asked.

"He's closeted, obviously," I said. "I'm just trying to get used to toning The Derek Show down a few notches, you know?

I think I can do it. I'm just too much of a rooster, sometimes. I want to crow, and I don't want to feel like there's a collar around my neck."

"Yeah, I can't see you doing that forever, but I guess you just have to play it out and see what happens," he said. "I guess it depends on what you want out of life. What's 'good,' and what's 'good enough,' and how long can you wait for it to get better?"

"I thought we weren't going to talk about me?" I smirked.

"Oops. My bad," he said, but I knew he meant well. In that moment I felt extra sorry for straight guys that couldn't imagine having a gay guy as a best friend. They were missing out.

We devoured our sushi and spent the rest of the lunch talking about movies and music. It's so good to spend time with a friend who just accepts you for who you are, with no judgement. We'd known each other forever, and that wasn't going to change.

After our second bottle of sake, we stumbled back to his place. I crawled into the comfy chair and he stretched out on the couch.

"What do you wanna do?" he asked.

"Netflix?" I said. "I think I need some *Always Sunny in Philadelphia*. Charlie is a freak."

"You got it." He turned the TV on and we let the remainder of the day slide by, with barely another word spoken.

17

A BUMP IN THE ROAD

"Swing by around 8 o'clock tonight?" said Luke, his hand resting on the doorframe of my classroom, once again. I was pretty sure that that was as physically close as he would ever get to me while we were on the school grounds.

"Yeah, sure," I said, smiling up at him. I decided to be brave. "I was thinking, maybe we could hit up a movie tonight?"

"I don't think that's such a good idea," he said.

"Luke, it's just a movie. No one can infer anything from us going to a movie together."

"Let's talk about that later, all right?" He was clearly frustrated with me, and I could see it. "See you at 8," and he walked down the hall.

We were spending more and more time together outside of school, and I was spending a few nights a week at his place, now. Mom was trying to ask questions without being too nosy, and Barry, I hoped, was keeping a lid on her sleuthing. Bammy was even worse. I knew she knew, and she hated feeling left out, but I had promised Luke I wouldn't include her, and so far I was keeping my promise. Tommy was just happy I was getting laid.

Me? I was deliriously happy, like a love-struck teenager. Even I knew it was obvious. But Luke and I had our own little trouble brewing, and we were each holding something back from one another. You're always careful at the beginning of a relationship to make sure you are aware of your partner's feelings. You don't want to push and you don't want to appear as crazy as you really are, but all of the tiptoeing leads to an eventual breakdown in communication. At some point you have to say what you really think and feel, otherwise there's no use in continuing.

It was clear to me that Luke and I needed to talk. As Tommy pointed out, I wasn't sure I was okay with just "good enough." I was frustrated that my boyfriend was afraid to be seen with me in public, and I could tell he wasn't ready to come out. I wasn't sure how much more patient I could be, though. We basically only saw each other at his house, and when we were at school he avoided me or treated me with this crazy macho persona that was standoffish, at best. I made a plan, and decided to see if I could pull it off tonight.

"Hey, handsome," I said, as he answered the door in a towel. "You are wearing far too many clothes."

He pulled me into his arms and kissed me. "Sorry, babe. Practice ran late and I wanted to get a quick shower in before you got here."

"Without me?" I said. "I could have joined you."

"Maybe later," he smirked, "if you're lucky. Go on and grab a seat in the kitchen. I have a bottle of wine open. There's some chili on the stove. Give it a stir for me and I'll be right out."

He stepped away from me, letting his towel slip just enough so I could see just the top of that amazing ass. That man knew what he was doing, all right. Yes, I would just have to be patient. But still, I knew we had to start somewhere.

He came out of his room with a pair of tight blue jeans on and a fresh t-shirt. "How's the wine?" he said.

"Good!" I handed him his glass. "Cheers, babe." I took a sip and judged the temperature of the room. He was smiling, I was smiling, dare I broach the subject again? "So, listen, I know you're being... cautious," I tried to choose my words carefully, "but I was really hoping we could go out tonight, after dinner. There's a little dive bar on the other side of town where we could go, and I'm sure no one would recognize us. We've spent every date night in, and I'd just like to get out with you, you know?"

He held his wine glass tightly in his hand. He had stopped smiling.

"Derek," he paused. "I don't know." He shook his head. "Where is this place?"

"It's this little dive bar," I started, hopefully. "The other side of downtown. Really, no one we know could possibly be there. It's totally off everyone's radar. It's called Bottom's Up."

He froze. Was there a reaction in his eyes?

"The gay bar?" he said. "No way. Not gonna happen." And that was it. End of discussion. I could feel him physically and mentally shutting down before my eyes.

"Luke, no one will see us."

"I'm not going there," he said, his voice rising slightly, "so you may as well stop asking."

"What's your damage, Heather?" I had to lighten the mood before this got out of hand.

"Enough with that 'Heather' shit, all right?" He slammed his glass down. Too late. He was angry. "I don't get your pop culture references. I don't watch RuPaul. I don't want to make out with you in public and I don't want to go to a gay bar to-night. I have my big game tomorrow, and tonight I just wanted to spend my time with you. Can we just sit down and eat, now?"

I took a deep breath. I went too far. Baby steps, Derek. Baby steps.

"Yeah, sure," I said. "No problem. It's probably not a good idea to go out before the Homecoming game, anyway. We need you to be fresh tomorrow, right?"

I reached over and kissed him. He didn't turn me away, but he didn't exactly melt in my arms.

"We're okay?" I asked.

"You know we are," he said, and he pulled my chair out for dinner.

But no, I didn't know anything. Nothing was certain. Was I fucking it up, after all?

18

GAME DAY

I woke up with Luke wrapped tight around me like a pretzel. At some point in the night I had became the "little spoon." I loved the feel of his arms holding me and the rise and fall of his chest against my back. I had to accept a few realities after last night's mini fight. Things were really progressing nicely, as long as I accepted the reality of the situation without pushing him. I loved spending time with him, but it was only good for him if we didn't acknowledge each other in public or go out together to a bar. Yet. But I had faith that that would change.

He began to stir, and I could feel his arms losing their grip, as his hands traveled across my back and a hundred little kisses covered my neck. Who needs a public affirmation when you have this? Or was I just lying to myself?

"Morning, babe," he said.

"*Mmmm*, nice." I did love those lips.

"Big day today," he said. "It's game day, remember?"

"How could I forget?" I said, and turned to look at him. "Bammy has had every class in school donating 'a few extra minutes' to make signs for the Homecoming. Are you nervous?"

"Nervous? No. Excited, yes. I feel confidant that we have a good team this year. I have a lot of really good seniors and just as many good junior players. No injuries. It's definitely not a 'rebuilding year' for us," he said. "I'm counting on us beating Billington this year. It's not like my job depends on it, but it sure would be nice."

"Well, if our coach is any example of the shape our team is in, we won't have any problem at all," I said, and kissed him, feeling the muscles in his arms. "Go, Commodores."

"Let's just hope it goes the right way. Shower?" He sat up.

"You bet, Coach." And we headed to the bathroom.

Luke and I drove separately to work. I made a stop to pick up coffee on my way, just to make sure I was a few minutes behind him. He hadn't said anything particularly paranoid, but I could feel that he was hyper aware of being seen together too much, so I wanted to make sure I did my best to ease his mind. Plus, I didn't want to throw his game off today, considering it was such an important game, indeed. We are always playing some type of game in life, aren't we?

"Good morning, Miss Mabel," I said as I walked into the reception area. "Is Bammy at her desk?"

"Now Derek, you know I can't keep track of all the comings and goings around here. That ain't my job," she said, without even looking up at me. "You know where her office is. Go find out yourself."

"Miss Mabel, don't you pretend that you aren't the one running the show around here," I said. "Some of us know better."

She half smiled at me with a quick glance and a raised eyebrow and then went back to her business, staring at her computer screen as if it was all going to make sense to her if she just pushed the right buttons. I saw her differently now, after Barry told me about her and Aunt Janey. I wondered about their story, but I was afraid that I could never ask. We just don't talk about those things, and our mutual silence on the subject was the most respectful way to proceed.

Bammy was at her desk as I knocked on her doorframe. "Grande latte, Miss Talbot?" I said.

"Oh, bless you, Derek!" she said, hand outstretched to grab the cup. "It has been insane around here this week. I just haven't had the time to take care of myself. I'm sure I look a right mess."

"You look beautiful," I said, as I took a seat opposite her desk.

"Oh, you liar. And you're not even trying to get into my pants." We laughed. "Speaking of which, are you ready to tell me whose pants you *have* been into, lately? Because don't think we haven't noticed you haven't been around too much. Tommy says for sure you've found a man, and Kit is just an eternal Moment of Silence. Did you bribe her, or something? What do you have on her?" She put the cup to her lips and carefully sipped.

I rolled my eyes and took a sip, myself. "No, nothing like that," I said. "Yes, there's someone, but I'm just not ready to talk about it, okay? I just need a little space on that." I tried to change the subject. "And I've just been keeping busy with Mom and Uncle Barry. It has been great catching up with them. And you know the Homecoming game isn't the only thing going on at school," I reminded her. "The musical goes up next weekend, in case you've forgotten."

"Of course not. And we are all just as excited about that as Homecoming," she lied, for my benefit. "It's just, you know. Football kinda rules the roost here."

"I do, indeed." And the football coach is ruling my roost, Bammy, and if you only knew just how much I wanted to tell you every detail. But I can't. Not yet.

"I'm just running to the salon to get my hair done after work," she continued "and then I'll be at the tailgate party in the parking lot at about 6 o'clock. See you then, I hope? Oh, and remember, Derek. Adult beverages are cool in the parking lot, but not in the bleachers. You're a teacher now, and you're representing the school."

"Go, Commodores," I said, and I took my coffee and headed to my classroom.

Homecoming is a pretty special thing in the South, and the high school was in full participation mode: posters on every wall, the majority of the students in Commodore colors, football players in their jerseys and letter jackets, cheerleaders in full uniform. I remember hating it all when I was a kid. I used to feel so awkward and left out. "Give them bread and circus," my history teacher had said, in disgust, cross-referencing our modern lust for football with the ancient Fall of Rome. But now, I have to admit, I was definitely getting into the team spirit, and I'm sure the fact that I was falling head over heels for our football coach had more than a little something to do with it.

The Booster Club and Band Moms organized a tailgate party in the main parking lot before the game. I had sent Luke a text message saying "Break a leg," but he hadn't responded. Can you use theatre jargon for sports, too? Anyway, I figured he was busy as hell getting the kids ready for the game, so I tried not to read too much into it.

I met Kit and Tommy in the parking lot. The weather had taken a sudden dip this past weekend, and we were all bundled in slightly heavier jackets and scarves. The alcohol we were about to consume was sure to warm us up, though.

"Hey there!" Tommy gave me a one-armed man hug. "All good?"

"All good," I said. "How about you?" Tommy was kind enough to know when to ask the right, easy questions, but to avoid the wrong, more difficult questions.

"Can't complain," he said. "Just busy with work and my girlfriend, you know." He smiled and handed me a beer from the trunk of his car. "Beer, Kit?"

"Oh, Tommy, you know I don't do carbs," Kit said. "Vodka soda, please."

"Coming right up," he said. Always the gentleman.

"So?" said Kit, looking at me as if she was saying everything by saying nothing.

I just smiled and winked at her while Tommy finished making her drink. She gave me a quick thumbs up while his back was still turned and then held on tight to my arm.

"Let's get our game on, y'all!" Tommy said, as he handed her a drink, disguised in the plastic confines of an adult sippy cup. The school had a firm "No Alcohol" rule in the stands, but like every other situation in the South, people just looked the other way, as long as we behaved.

Bammy sent us a text message to say she was on her way, and it wasn't long before she joined us in the bleachers, just as the kick off began. The crowd was cheering and the stands were shaking with the rumbling of stomping shoes. Everyone was on their feet, paying close attention to the game, yelling their support. It was a crisp autumn night, and the air smelled of popcorn and hot dogs. I could see Luke down by the sidelines, surrounded by his assistant coaches and the players on the bench. He never looked up at me, but I imagined that he knew I was there, supporting him. I couldn't wait to congratulate him on a job well done, as soon as we beat Billington.

"We've got spirit, yes we do! We've got spirit, how 'bout you?!" The cheerleaders yelled and high kicked from the sidelines, getting the crowd riled up. We scored quickly in the first quarter, and just never looked back.

"Go, Commodores!" I yelled, popcorn flying from the bucket in my hands as I jumped up and down like a fool.

"It's great to see you with such spirit, Derek!" said Bammy. "I don't remember you liking football so much."

"Oh, I've always loved football," I said. "I just like it a bit more now than I used to." Whoa, Derek. Slow down on that drinking. It won't be long before Miss Vice Principal catches on. Loose lips, you know.

Kit just smiled and took another sip of her secret vodka and soda from the plastic cup that Tommy had given her.

The band put on a great show during half time, and we were all feeling fine, singing and dancing in the stands. Even Bammy loosened up and started drinking from our cups. The effects of a winning game and secret alcohol were catching up with all of us, and the team did not disappoint in the second half, either. Luke and his team were definitely on their way to beating Billington, there was no doubt about that.

The crowd was pumped up beyond belief as our quarterback threw the winning touchdown and brought the game to a close. I was so proud as I watched Luke and the Billington coach meet mid field and shake hands.

"That's my man!" I yelled.

"What did you say?" said Bammy. Kit stared at me, wide eyed, and Tommy was, thankfully, on his phone with Meredith, making plans for later.

"*Our* man, I meant." *Shit.* "That's our man! A fine coach. Yep." I put my cup to my lips and looked away, hoping she would not question me further.

"Derek Walter, you are the worst liar ever," Bammy said. "But we're both a little tipsy, so I'm just gonna pretend that I didn't hear that."

"Come on, y'all," said Kit, saving the day. "It's time to go celebrate."

"I just think we should tell the coach he did a great job," I said.

"Derek, I don't think that's a good idea," said Kit. "We need to head on out, now." She tugged me by the arm like a child, but I pulled away gently.

"I'll meet y'all at the car," I said. "I won't do anything crazy. I promise."

"Well that cat's officially out of the bag," said Bammy. "Kit, I think you need to catch me up on some stuff. Derek, I know we can't stop you, but please don't do anything stupid. We'll be at the car."

I walked into the steady stream of the football zombies as we pushed on down the stairs of the stadium stands. I was drunk and I knew it, but I was also focused. I wasn't doing anything wrong. I'm a greyhound. I just wanted to see Luke. I just wanted to tell him congratulations. Nothing wrong with that. Why are my friends acting so bizarre?

I spotted him down by the sidelines, surrounded by an adoring crowd. A school photographer was taking his picture with the quarterback, and there were back slaps and high fives all around. His father, Red Walcott, was standing proudly at his side.

"Luke!" I yelled, but he didn't seem to notice. "Luke!" I pushed in further and forced myself into his line of sight. He just looked up at me, distractedly, and his smile faded.

"Hey! Luke! Great game!" I said, too loudly. "Congratulations!" Not thinking, I reached up to hug him, but his arms stayed at his side, and he quickly pulled back.

"Thank you for your support, Mr. Walter," one arm extended to my shoulder, keeping me a safe distance from him. And he turned and put his back to me, as he walked further into the crowd of excited supporters. Red looked at me strangely, and I could feel instantly that I had made the wrong move.

I felt like an idiot as I stood there, alone. The crowd shuffled along, following our winning coach towards the exit. Had I gone too far? All I did was try to hug him? Men hug, right? Should I not have done that? What was he thinking now?

Shit. Go, Commodores.

19

LET'S PUT ON A SHOW

The next week was miserable.

I fucked up, and I knew it. In his eyes I may as well have proclaimed our eternal homosexual love in front of God and country, or at least that's what I imagined he thought. I had to make it all up in my head, as he wasn't speaking to me, at all. I sent him an apology text after the game, but he didn't respond, of course. The next morning, I realized I had sent three messages, which was three too many. I know some genius out there must have invented an app that won't let you text message if you've had too many drinks, right? I needed to find one, yesterday. Hello, Silicon Valley. Don't drink and dial!

By now, Bammy and Tommy knew everything, as it was obvious as hell. I gave Kit the go ahead to tell them the whole story, but I couldn't face the situation myself. I didn't want to talk about it. I wanted to stay in bed and crawl under the sheets and die. Unfortunately, I couldn't. As an adult with a job, I had responsibilities, so I threw myself full force into my work. This was tech week, and show time was Saturday, so we had a lot of work to do on the musical.

I didn't see Luke at all in the teachers' lounge on Monday. I'm sure he was avoiding me, and the pit in my stomach grew larger every morning as I approached the school. This felt worse than any crush I had ever had as a teenager. When I finally did spot him walking towards me, I tried to catch his eye, but he just powered through, as if his conversation with the pretty blond science teacher was the most interesting thing he'd heard all week. He was out to prove something, and if he hurt me in the process, well so be it.

Damn it, Luke. Yes, I made a mistake, but now will you look at the mistake you are making? Do not lose me. We are good together.

I spent my nights working on the show. I was really proud of the kids. They had so much talent, and their hard work was paying off, considering the small budget for the Arts Program we were allotted by the school district. Bammy, Kit and Tommy were coming to support us on opening night, as well as Mom and Uncle Barry.

But, Luke? After four days of silence, I caved. I called. The phone rang four times and then went to voice mail, so I knew he wasn't on the phone. He just wasn't going to take a call from me.

"Hey, it's me. But you know that," I started, unsure of what to say, even though I had rehearsed it four times. It all went out the window the second I heard the beep. "I just wanted to say I'm sorry. I just, I don't know... I fucked up. I should have let you have your moment and just praised you from afar, like everyone else. But babe, I was so proud of you, and I wanted to tell you. I wanted to stand by your side. And I know now that that was stupid. Well, not stupid. Just misguided. Just a really bad choice, fueled by hormones and adult beverages. But I did it, and I'm so sorry. I really am. And the last few days have just been awful. I miss you like hell, and I just wanted you to know that. I wish we could talk this out, and I hope I'll hear back from you. I really do. Because, you know... I have your socks. And I have to return those." And I stopped. I was silly, now. Lame. Rambling the lovesick song of a tortured teenager. I honestly didn't know if I was making it worse, but at this point I had nothing to lose. "So... can we talk soon? My show is tomorrow, Friday. I hope you can come." And I hung up.

Thursday night I tossed and turned, unable to sleep. I missed his arms, his smell. My brain and heart were in turmoil, and I had no solution. Friday after school I camped out in the auditorium, too busy with last minute notes for the show to worry about my love life, and I was grateful for the distraction. Mom and Uncle Barry came to meet me back stage just before the curtain was about to rise.

"Hey there sweetie, are you nervous?" Mom said, as she gave me a hug.

"Oh, you know how I am," I said. "The nerves fuel the energy. But these kids are good. Great, even. I'm so proud of them. They've worked so hard on this."

"Well, they have you to thank for that. I'm sure we'll enjoy it," she said. "Come on Barry, let's go find our seats and leave this boy to his business."

"I'll be along in a second, dear," he said, and she nodded and wandered off through the door. "Hey, Dolly," he said, looking at me quizzically. "What's up? Something went wrong, didn't it?"

"Horribly," I nodded. "I pushed too far. I'm pretty sure I scared him away for good."

"Well, remember what I said. If that's his choice, then it's his to make. He may just realize what he's missing and come around. But there's nothing you can do about it right now. The show must go on! Break a leg. We're proud of you, Derek." He squeezed my arm and turned to go find Mom.

I peaked through the curtain as the Stage Manager called places. I could see Bammy, Kit, Tommy, Mom, Uncle Barry... and no Luke. I didn't expect him to come, but much like that time I ran an extra lap at the lake, I was cashing in all my wishes, hoping the heavens would prove me wrong.

The show went off without any major disasters. We had a dancer slip and fall onstage during "Hand Jive," but she got right back up and kept going. A few light cues didn't go exactly as planned, but no one forgot their lines, and the kids sounded amazing. The curtain came down and they all gathered on stage for their final bow to receive their praise from their family and friends.

I clapped hard from the safety of stage right as the kids were showered with well-deserved accolades and a standing ovation. My Sandy and Danny walked down center stage, arm in arm, and held their hands up to quiet the crowd.

"Thank you, thank you so much!" they said. "We'd just like to say a special thanks to someone we couldn't have done this without. We are so happy you are our teacher, director, and biggest supporter. Mr. Walter, come on out and give a bow. Can we make some noise for Mr. Walter?!"

Blushing, but thrilled, I walked out onstage to give my two leads a hug, then turned to wave at the audience as they applauded. The follow spot was directly on me, and with the bright lights I could barely make out any faces in the crowd, but I could see someone walking swiftly from the very back of the auditorium, down the center aisle. As they approached nearer to the stage, I could see that it was a man carrying a huge bouquet of flowers that obscured his face. I started to sweat as he got closer and closer. Did he really come? Did he bring me flowers?!

"*Bravo!*" he said, as he thrust the bouquet up towards me, and I bent down to take them from his hands.

My heart was pounding. It was David.

20

TOGETHER, AGAIN?

Everything around me was happening in slow motion.

I had the flowers in my hand and David was staring up at me, grinning from ear to ear. The audience was clapping and the Stage Manager was signaling for us to step back, as the final curtain was about to come down. We took a few steps backwards and the kids erupted in wild cheers backstage, patting each other on the back and hugging. They were beyond pumped, and they deserved to experience every second of that joy. They earned it.

But I couldn't breathe. David? Oh, God, what is happening? What is he doing here?

I walked towards stage right with the enormous bouquet and leaned against the far wall, before the entrance to the dressing rooms. The kids were so high on life and so busy with each other that they hardly noticed me anymore. I had to go out there, right? I had to face him? And my friends. And explain this. But I couldn't explain this. I just wanted to hide and hope that someone else would clean up my mess. Again. David, what are you doing?

I took three deep breaths and headed towards the exit, into the main auditorium. David was already standing near my mom and Uncle Barry. He had met them both in New York once, when they came to visit, but this was his first time meeting the Scooby Gang. As I approached, Barry saw me out of the corner of his eye and gave me a strange, uncomfortable smile, eyebrows arched dramatically. Psychically, he was telling me *Just get through this, Dolly. Figure it out as it comes. Be strong.* I gave a subtle nod, took another breath and walked up to them.

"Oh, honey, it was fantastic," my mom said, kissing me on the cheek.

"Well done, kid," Uncle Barry added. "You made us proud, as always."

Kit, Bammy and Tommy gathered round to kiss and hug me, as well. David stood a little off to the side a bit, uncharacteristically quiet, but smiling his Cheshire Cat grin.

"Drinks at The Firelight?" said Bammy, breaking the tension. "I think we all deserve it after the last two weeks, don't you?" Everyone was ignoring the elephant in the room, but this was one situation I had to take care of, on my own.

"You guys go ahead," I said. "I'll be along soon."

"Well, us old fogies are heading home." Barry chimed in. "Your mom and I have an appointment with a nightcap and our beds. It was a pleasure seeing you again, David." Always the proper Southerner. "Have fun, kids."

They all turned to leave, and I stood there frozen, unsure of what to say or do or think or feel. David was standing there, silent, with a contented smile on his face, hands folded in front of him like he was having a hard time containing his excitement. I could feel it. But at the same time, he was cautiously aware that I was trying not to freak out.

"Hi, Derek," he said.

"Hey. That was a… surprise." I was unsure of what to say.

"A good one, I hope?" He was so proud of himself, he was bouncing.

"Yeah, sure, it's just… well, we haven't really spoken since we, since I…" I stopped short of saying it.

"Since you abandoned me on a moving 4 train, on our way to get our Marriage License?" he said. Oh, shit. Here it comes. "No, Derek, we haven't spoken since then. But here's the thing. It's okay. What you did, I forgive you. I'm here to tell you I forgive you. I've been meeting with my therapist. You know Gerald? You remember Gerald? Well, Gerald says this is a classic case of someone acting out. You just needed to tell me what you felt, and you couldn't say it. You did it the best way you could. I was smothering you. I get that! I was pushy. But you know me, Derek. I push with love! I meant well. I mean, we'd spent so many years together, of course planning a wedding seemed like the logical next step. Who cares about the Supreme Court, right? I mean, we're in love! But that was my dream, Derek, and I pushed you into it. I know that now. I can be a force of nature, believe you me, I get that. HA! I should have my own reality show. That would be a hoot, right?! Can you imagine? *Me* on TV? But I've thought about it, and I don't need that. The marriage, I mean. (I'd *love* the TV show!) I don't need the ring, or the big wedding, and God knows we have enough stuff. I mean, can you imagine all those gifts? Yes, they'd be amazing, our friends have such good taste, of course. I mean, you've seen Marcos's apartment, right? Amazing! But do we really need all that stuff? We could barely fit in our two small apartments as it was, we were gonna have to move to Brooklyn to afford a big enough place for all of that. And these days, we can't even afford Brooklyn. HA! The hipsters ran the prices up. And I'm NOT living in Jersey. Ever! But I don't want all that stuff, anyway. So I sat down with Gerald and figured it all out. I'm much better now, Derek. Trust me. Much better. *Calmer.* Centered. Can't you tell? I mean, I feel like I radiate calm now, you know? You can feel it, right? So I was gonna call, but that felt so awkward, so impersonal. I went online and looked it up and lo and behold, Mr. Walter's a teacher! Thank God this school has a website, right? Otherwise I wouldn't have seen it. I wouldn't have known. And *Grease?!* We both loved *Grease!* It was a sign, I just knew it. So I talked it over with Gerald and Marcos, and they both agreed. I had to do it! I booked a ticket and *voila!* Here I am."

"Here you are." I smiled, meekly. Is this a dream? Am I still on stage? Someone please hand me my script, because I've forgotten my lines.

"And here's the thing," he continued. "Derek, we had a good thing going. And I want that back. I want *you* back. Now, I don't expect you to pack your bags and jump on a plane with me tonight. That would be amazing, of course, but I'm not asking for that. So, listen, I've checked into the best little boutique hotel I could find in this *charming* little town of yours and I'm staying here all next week. Now, I don't want to pressure you, I know you have things to think about. And if you need to get on the phone with Gerald, you just say the word. He can do video chat sessions with us too, of course. He's very digital. Very savvy. A genius. He's *so* good. Trust me. But right now I just want you to know I'm here. I'm here, Derek. *I care.* I do. I really do. And I'm ready to start all over again. Waddya say?"

What DO I say? Oh, God, what do I say?

"I… I… yeah." I could feel the walls pressing in. "Yeah. We can talk. Tomorrow. Right now, I just need… I just need to think. I'll call you. Tomorrow."

And I turned to leave, shell-shocked. David is my past. Sure, it would be easy to step back into that life. Comfortable. But that's just going through the motions. I need to stop looking for my happiness in others. I need to find it in myself. That's why you came back home, Derek. But what about Luke? I can't live in the closet again, like Uncle Barry. So I turn back to David, because it's easy? Is that really a possibility?

■ ■ ■

I got into my car and stared out the windshield into the night. There was only one thing I could do, so I picked up the phone and dialed.

"Kit, it's me."

"Oh, baby, we were so worried! *Where. Are. You?* We're at The Firelight waiting for you. And gossiping like hell, of course. But just 'cause we love you. You know that."

"I do. I know." I said. "But I don't think I can drink tonight. Or at least, I shouldn't drink tonight. I just need my friends. All of you. Can we meet at Tommy's? He has the best couch."

"You got it, baby," she said. "We're on our way. I just need to pull Bammy away from this guy at the bar. But there's no way she's going home with him, anyway. He's way too alternative for her. Not enough khaki for her in here, tonight, and she had to make do with what was on special, you know?"

"Oh, Kit, I adore you, you know that? I'm on my way."

I don't really remember getting on the interstate, or driving downtown. It's as if Willie was on autopilot, and he just knew the way. People talk about muscle memory when it comes to working out, but I had muscle memory during emotional breakdowns, though I wish that weren't the case. I'd had far too much practice with tears and second-guessing myself when it came to relationships. Why can't this be easier?

I pressed the elevator button and rode the three flights up to Tommy's apartment. I could have taken the stairs, but I didn't want to exert any more energy than necessary. I just wanted to collapse and moan and have my friends tell me what to do, because I couldn't think for myself right now.

Tommy opened the door and gave me a big hug as I walked in. "Hey, man. Kit and Bammy are in the kitchen," he said. "They have a surprise for you."

We walked together down the hall and to the left, and there it was, on the table. Ben and Jerry's ice cream. Chunky Monkey, New York Super Fudge Chunk, Cherry Garcia, Cookie Dough. They had all my favorites. I looked up at them and I could feel my face fall as the tears welled up in my eyes.

"*Oooh*, baby, no!" said Kit, as she rushed forward with Bammy, both of them hugging me tight. "Let's get some sugar into you and you'll feel better. Which one do you want?"

"All of them," I sniffled. "Everything. Just put it all in a big ass bowl. Thanks, y'all. I really love you."

"We love you too, Derek," said Bammy. "You know we're here for you. Now go get settled on the couch. We'll be right in."

Tommy was waiting for me in the living room. I took a seat in the big stuffy oversized chair, flung my legs over the edge and let my head drop back.

"*Blaaaaaaaah*," I said. "I have no clue what I've done. My relationships seem to be a never-ending study in failure. Why does this shit happen to me?"

"Well, the way I see it," he said as the girls walked back into the room, "you haven't really done anything wrong. You tried with David, you tried with Luke. You have guts, man."

"Or I'm just stupid," I said.

"Well, there's that." Tommy smiled. "Though I'd say you're more of a hopeless romantic… with a learning disability. But you know what? Here's the truth. You get knocked down, but you get up again, and you keep trying. I admire you for that. So, now you just need to decide what to do next. No sense beating yourself up over the past."

"He's *so* right," said Bammy, offering me a ginormous bowl of ice cream. "Even though that speech made me want to sing Chumbawamba. But he's right. And that's why we're here. We can help. Let's assess the situation." Always the planner, that girl.

Bammy suggested that first we define where I currently stood with each guy, Luke and David, and then we discuss the pros and cons for each. We started with David, since he had most recently popped back into the picture so dramatically.

"Well, the current situation is this," I began. "David and I dated for almost five years in New York, which is considered an eternity there. Couples never last that long, and if they do, they get married. But I freaked. He was smothering me, and honestly, I wasn't sure I liked who I had become in those five years. It was a true case of 'It's not you, it's me.' So I broke it off and came back here. Since then, I feel much more grounded, and being with all of you has made me feel really Southern again, and I like that. It feels good.

I took a big bite of ice cream, and continued. "Pros and cons? Well, the pros with David are that we spent five years together, and he knows my moods pretty damn well. He makes me laugh, we have a ton of friends in common, though they seem closer to him, than me. He introduces me to new things, he's a foodie, and the sex was good, albeit a bit 'normal' towards the end. And I know he loves me. I never doubted that. The cons? He's quite the personality. He can be pushy, use up all of the oxygen in the room, and really rub people the wrong way, even though I know it's unintentional. He's not a good listener, and he's fairly opinionated. But, he says he's changed. And I believe, at least, that he's working on it."

"Good," said Bammy. "Keep going."

"And Luke? Wow. Luke," I said, "is like no one I've ever been with. When I came back here, I hated him on sight. I wanted to blame him for how I hated myself when I was growing up. He took all of that in stride, and pushed me to really give him a chance, in ways I hadn't before with anyone else, while at the same time he was opening up to me. But I pushed him too far, and now, well, we aren't anywhere. We never actually defined 'us' at all."

The bowl was cold in my hand, so I set it down on the coffee table. "The pros? Well, he's damn handsome. Pretty much my golden unicorn. That straight guy who isn't straight, who I lusted after for years. He makes me feel warm and safe and protected, somehow. He's ridiculously friendly, smart, athletic, and a great cook. The sex with him hasn't progressed 'all the way,' if you know what I mean, but it's incredibly passionate, and I have no doubts it would just get better. He knows my friends, and understands what it means to have grown up here. We can share that understanding. The cons? Well, there's that big Southern closet, to begin with. He doubts himself, doubts the reaction his family and friends would have if they knew the truth about him. He's afraid, and that's hard to watch. I know he likes me. A lot. But he wants to keep me trapped in his house, and I need to breathe. I want to be seen with him, and not just pretend that we are friends or acquaintances. And I'm not sure when he will be ready for that, if ever. The thing is, I walked away from David, and now Luke just walked away from me. The irony isn't lost on me."

We all took a pause, and just stared at each other for a minute, each of our brains working overtime, trying to figure out the right thing to say to make sense of this jumbled situation.

"It's okay," I said. "This helped. I know what to do. I love you guys."

I stood up, grabbed my jacket and walked out the door.

21

IN OR OUT?

I walked up to his door and rang the bell out of habit, but I was startled when it actually made a sound. He had fixed it. That made me smile, but then I remembered why I was there, and my smile faded as the nervousness grew inside of me.

I heard footsteps, then a pause.

"Luke? It's Derek. Please. Can I come in?"

I heard the lock *click*, and for a second I wasn't sure if he was locking or unlocking it, so when the light from the living room spilled out across the doorframe into the darkness of the night I almost began to cry again, but I knew I had to keep it together.

"Hey," I said, raising my eyebrows and managing a half-hearted smile.

"Hey," he mumbled. He opened the door wider and stepped back, allowing me to enter, then shut it quickly behind him and leaned against it, looking downward as he stuffed his fists into the pockets of his jeans.

"Thanks for letting me in."

"No problem," he said, but I wasn't sure he was telling the truth.

"I... damn, Luke. I've missed you."

He didn't say anything or even look up at me. He just kept staring at his shoes, the muscles in his jaw clenching with every breath. I had to say something quick or I was out the door in thirty seconds. This was my only shot, and it had better be good.

"I guess you got my message," I started. "But I just wanted to tell you in person. I'm sorry. I really am. If I pushed too hard and crossed a line, that was my mistake. And I own that. But the thing is, you and I have something special. Something I've never felt with anyone before. You're in my head every day. Part of me knows I should walk away, while another part of me wants to grab you, throw you down and kiss the hell out of you. We both felt something huge in our lives for the last few weeks, and I think we can both acknowledge that. But I miss you, and I can't handle this silence that is between us now. So here's the thing. Nothing will happen between us, if *we* don't want it to, or don't try. Everything *can* happen between us, if we *both* want it to, and we *do* try. The passion, the conversations, the touching, the kisses, the scent, the words, the time we have spent together. That has been my everything. *You* have been my everything. Luke, you are thinking far, far too hard. If you want a true partner, he is right in front of you. I could list every reason why you should be with me, but truthfully, you know them already. With bravery, we can make reality. With hesitation, other choices cement themselves. I miss the hell out of you. I don't want to sleep alone, anymore. You mean so much to me, Luke."

I felt like I had put it all out there, thrown everything down on the line. I did my best and opened my heart fully to him. But the tension in the room did not diminish, as I had hoped it would.

He continued to stare down at his feet, and his face didn't change. I couldn't read him right now. I didn't know if anything I had said had any effect on him, whatsoever. My heart started pounding even harder, and I could feel the moment slipping from my fingers. I felt like the Bachelor, and my rose was about to be rejected.

He looked up and locked onto my eyes. He spoke, softly, but with purpose. "I felt free with you, Derek. Like I could do anything. Be anyone." He took a breath. "But I'm not like you. We're not at the same place in our lives. This is still all new to me. I'm not ready to tell my family, to stand up in front of the school... in front of my athletes. My team. I just, I.." He paused. "I can't be the guy you want me to be," he said. "I can't be the guy you deserve."

My stomach was caught in my throat, and I started to shake. I wanted to cry, but I was holding everything in. There was nothing more to say, really. I could hear Kit in my head reminding me that confidence was sexy. Right now the only thing I was confident about was the fact that I needed to leave. Immediately. He made a choice. He was clear about it, and the longer I stayed or tried to convince him otherwise the more pathetic I would look.

I walked closer to him and he stood there, motionless. I reached up and kissed him softly on his cheek, one hand on his chest, the other on his shoulder. There was no reaction. The smell of his neck made my knees weak, but that was just an unfortunate memory at this point.

"You're an amazing man," I said. "I hope you find your happiness."

And I walked out the door without looking back.

22

A FISH OUT OF WATER

"You call this a bagel?" said David. "How can they call this a bagel? This isn't a bagel. My god. It's basically a salty donut. How can you people live on these things? Oh, right. We should just cover it in bacon. Or cheese. *Ooh!* Or deep-fry it! You people love to deep fry things. I've never seen so many things deep-fried in my entire life. Cheese, Twinkies, Oreo cookies, candy bars. Even turkeys! What'll they think of next? Deep fried pickles?"

"We already have that," I said, half smiling. It was strange sitting here with David, as if I was watching a foreign movie, but laughing at all the wrong times. We were on our way to finding our rhythm again, but did I even want that? I wasn't sure, yet.

"Of course you do!" said David as he placed the rejected bagel back down on his plate. "And this coffee? These people should be arrested. I can't deny it's cheap. That's a plus. I mean, $1 for an endless cup of coffee? It's insane. Where's their profit? But the look on her face when I asked for a tall iced skinny caramel macchiato was amazing. Priceless. Hello? It's as if I was speaking another language or something! I swear, I don't know how you people drink this stuff. It's basically brown water! I will never get used to it here."

You won't have to, I thought to myself, as I gazed out the window.

It was a beautiful autumn day, with winter just around the corner. It had been a few weeks since I made my last ditch effort with Luke, and so much had changed. David and I were having a Saturday morning breakfast at Margie's Lunch Counter, downtown. Margie's was a throwback to another era, and I loved it. Vintage wood paneling from the 1940s, counter tops with specks of glitter, vinyl seats and circular booths and amazingly cheap breakfast and lunch specials with Southern favorites like grits, okra and fried green tomatoes. The waitresses were all older ladies of another generation, with names like Bertha, Madge and Ethel. It wasn't quite David's cup of tea, but I was trying to expose him to the "real people" culture that I loved so much in Parkville.

After showing up on opening night, David had been persistent. Not pushy, but persistent. More than I thought he could be, actually, and that's saying a lot. He really kept his eye on the prize. Maybe I learned how to be a greyhound from him? That first week he was in Parkville we met a few times before he headed back to New York. We just had a simple coffee, then a walk by the lake. Our conversations were tough and awkward, but I could feel that he was trying. I kept him away from my family and friends, because I really needed to see for myself how I felt. Had he really changed? What if I had I changed too much?

Things progressed very slowly, at first. I was impressed with his patience. After that first week, he sent me a few text messages from New York, and we just started talking again, more every day. Soon we were spending a few nights a week video chatting. Though I resisted his attempts at a group therapy session with Gerald, every now and then Marcos would jump onscreen with him, and that was nice to see a familiar face. There was a hole in my heart where Luke had been, and I didn't expect that David would be the one to fill it, but I was surprised at how easily we fell back into our old routines. Not in a bad way, but in a comfortable way. David was like that old sweater you rediscover when you are switching your summer closet for your winter one. You put it on after months of forgetting that it even existed, and it just feels good. It felt right. It was easy. Easier than I thought it could be, post Luke.

Soon after, he started flying down here every two weeks and spending long weekends, getting to know my friends, my town, my life. He looked exactly as I'd left him. Model thin, dark hair, trendy wire framed glasses, impeccably dressed in shades of black and grey. He was the anti-Luke. He didn't fit in at all, but rather than find it awful and awkward, it made me laugh. He kept referring to everyone as "you people," no matter how many times I tried to get him to say "y'all." It just sounded so funny coming from his lips. He complained about everything; the unhealthy food, the lack of fashion sense, the over reliance on cars. He was a true New Yorker, lost in the South. We were from different worlds, but somehow we had found each other, drifted apart, and then slowly, cautiously, been reunited.

And the one thing that about David that made me happier than anything else? He was out. Out and proud. In a land of Republicans he was capital "G" Gay, and he didn't give two shits if people sneered, commented or even noticed us at all. He was fearless, and after spending so many nights hiding behind walls with Luke, I felt free again.

"Next time I come down here I am bringing you bagels," he said. "Real bagels. I honestly don't know how you have survived. And sourdough? There's just no decent Jewish deli in this town, right?"

"Well, we used to have one, but it's a sushi place now. They put matzah balls in the egg drop soup. Long story." I laughed. "We have other things that are better, though. You learn to adjust."

"Well, I'll tell you what," he said. "When it comes to desserts, I'll have to agree with you there. I mean, there's no rugelach, but these pies? Oh, my god. Pecan pie, blueberry pie, banana cream pie. Chess pie? I'd never heard of it before and now it's all I ever want for my coffee break. We just have to find a better place for coffee! Please tell me there's better coffee, somewhere?"

"Hey, I have an idea," I said. "Since you're heading back to New York tomorrow, let's go out tonight for some fun. I'll show you Parkville's burgeoning gay side of town, and we'll have a few laughs. Okay?"

"Derek, darling, I put myself in your capable hands," he said. "I trust you." He leaned across the table and gave me a kiss, right in front of Margie, Bertha, Madge and Ethel.

I can honestly say it's starting to feel nice to be with David again. One closet door closes, and another closet door comes flying open, right?

23

A GAY OLD TIME

"This is disgusting," said David. "I feel like I'm in a redneck version of the East Village."

"Welcome to Bottom's Up," I said as we walked into the bar. "Isn't it great?!"

"Do we need to get shots before we come in here?" he said. "I feel like we need shots. Like, hepatitis and Ebola and Black Death. Do they ever clean this place? Oh, my god. My mother would die."

"Let's hope your mother doesn't show up here," I said. "That would be awkward." He laughed, but he was still holding tight to my side with both hands, as if he needed protection. "Let's get a few drinks and you'll feel better. What are you in the mood for?"

"Some disinfectant?"

"Funny." I pointed in the corner. "Tell you what, go grab that table over there and I'll get the first round." I paused, and then turned back to him. "But be careful of the inmates. They may bite."

"Now who's being a smart ass?" he said, reaching over to give me a kiss. "Make sure there's vodka in it. Lots. At least that will kill any germs in the glass."

He wandered over to the table by the jukebox and took a seat, looking around at the patrons as if he had just landed on another planet and he was sent there to analyze their behavior. He cracked me up, but sometimes I felt like I was dating Felix from *The Odd Couple*.

"Hey there," I said to the bartender. "How y'all doing tonight?"

"Can't complain," he said. "What can I do ya for?"

"A pitcher of Long Island Ice Tea, please, and 4 shots of Jack."

The bartender grabbed a pitcher and multiple bottles and started concocting a mess of liquor that I have never really understood. How can so many disparate tastes come together to make something so undeniably awesome?

"That'll be $16, buddy," he said.

I laughed a little to myself. Sixteen whole dollars? How could I ever think of leaving this place? I handed him a twenty and took the pitcher back to our table. David was staring wide eyed at every detail of the bar, including the patrons.

"I never knew there were so many uses for duct tape," he said.

"Yep. I think there's even a blog. We can look it up online it later." I handed him a shot of whiskey and poured out two Long Island Ice Teas. "Here's to us. Who's like us?"

"Damn few!" he said, and we downed our first shot. We laughed. It was a line from a Stephen Sondheim musical called *Merrily We Roll Along.* Something I could never have laughed about with Luke. I felt a slight pang in my heart, but it was true. He never would have gotten the reference. With David, it all just came easy.

The drinks started to kick in, and David was relaxing more and more. It took some time, but I think he actually started to enjoy himself. The two twinks next to us took over the jukebox, and the sounds of Britney filled the air.

"Where y'all from?" one of them said to us, over the strains of "Oops, I Did it Again."

"A place where we don't end our sentences in prepositions," David laughed. I almost spit out my drink. "I've always wanted to say that! I saw that on an episode of *Designing Women* years ago. Julia Sugarbaker! Oh, my god! I love this place!" His vodka was kicking in.

"I don't get it," said the twink, and we just laughed and laughed.

"Come on," I said, after we had finished our drinks. "Let's get out of here. I have another surprise for you."

The Bears' Club wasn't that far from Bottom's Up, and we were there and parked in no time at all. I hadn't called Uncle Barry, but I didn't think he'd be too upset. I had told David about Barry/Beret, but he hadn't seen the full drag experience, yet. I figured now was as good a time as any.

We walked through the back entrance and the red lacquer door shut behind us. I didn't see Scotty in his usual spot, so he must have been fetching drinks for Beret. We crept over to the stage, but there weren't any performers. We must have arrived in between shows, or maybe they were just having a meeting and cocktails tonight? Who knows?

"Come on," I said. "Beret's dressing room is downstairs. Follow me."

"I love this!" said David. "I feel like I'm stepping back into time. This is, like, *so* Southern underground culture. *Midnight in the Garden of Good and Evil.* Amazing!"

We walked slowly down the stairs and I could see light coming from Beret's room. She had the door closed, so she's either getting ready or enjoying an after performance cocktail. I tapped on the door but opened it at the same time, without waiting for an answer. That was a mistake.

Beret was standing in the middle of her room, in full sequined regalia. There was a man in a grey pinstripe suit with his back to me, his arms around her in a full embrace. He didn't turn around.

"Derek!" Beret was surprised. "Close that door this instant!"

"Wait," said David over my shoulder. "What's going on?"

I slammed the door shut. "We need to leave," I said. "Now."

"But I didn't see her," he said. "I didn't see anything. *No fun!*"

I did. I saw everything. Especially the reflection of the man in the suit in her vanity mirror.

It was Red Walcott, Luke's father.

24

THANKSGIVING

Thanksgiving was coming up and it was my absolute favorite holiday. The food was the best, and I loved getting together with all the people who meant the most to me. I'd invited the Scooby Gang, but Tommy was going to Memphis to spend time with Meredith's extended family. They had courageously taken the next step, so unfortunately they couldn't come. David had flown down from New York the night before. We had officially been back together now for several weeks, and he hadn't pressured me into making any decisions, but I knew that I had something to say tonight. I only hoped everyone was ready.

Luke and I had fallen into a casual nothingness. I occasionally saw him in the hallways or during the Monday meetings, but I felt nothing. Or at least I convinced myself of that. It had taken plenty of time to get over him, but when someone tells you to your face that there's no chance, you lose hope quickly and come to terms with reality. David was my reality now.

Mom was in the kitchen putting all the final touches together. It was going to be a full traditional spread; turkey, stuffing, cranberry sauce, mashed potatoes, gravy, candied yams, green bean casserole with the little toasted onions, deviled eggs and garlic rolls. She even made her famous peach cobbler for dessert. Just wait until David tried that! I was practically already falling asleep just thinking about the meal ahead. Screw the carbs. Today was an official cheat day.

Bammy and Kit arrived, bottles of wine and extra desserts in hand, and we sat down to watch the parade, live from New York. I missed that city so much. I thought about her every day since I left. People kept asking me "How could you leave New York?" "I thought my story was done there," I'd say. But maybe it wasn't?

David came down the stairs in an atrocious holiday sweater that we found at the mall. He thought it was hysterical and terribly ironic, but no one was comfortable enough with him yet to get in on his fashion joke. I knew they liked him. They had to, because they loved me. But there was still a bit of tiptoeing around him. It would take some time for the Yankee to fit in, but he had been really patient with me, so I owed him my patience, as well.

"Hi, Bammy! You look beautiful!" he said. "And Kit, so stylish, as always. You would definitely fit in in the City," and he kissed her on both cheeks in the European style. "Where's Tommy?"

"He's in Memphis," I said. "With Meredith's family."

"I hate Memphis," said Bammy, reaching for a carrot stick and dipping it into the Ranch dressing. "Everything is grey, or Elvis."

We all laughed as we watched the Underdog float head down Broadway. David was squeezed in next to me in the big cushy chair, one arm around me, his other hand holding a mug of coffee and Baileys.

"Remember when we used to go watch them get the balloons ready for the parade?" I said.

"Do I ever. Oh, my god, *this* one," and he pointed to me, "would get my ass out of bed at four in the morning to hike over to the Upper West Side. The Upper West Side! Behind the American Museum of Natural History. That's where they blow up the big floats before the parade. Such a kid. He got such a kick out of it. You were like a kid with a behind the scenes ticket to the circus! So fun to watch. You light up so much when you're happy. You know that? That's why I love you so much." He smiled and looked at me, expectedly.

I hadn't said it, yet. The "L" word. It was coming, I knew it, but it still wasn't time. I reached over and kissed him on the nose and hoped the moment would pass without too much speculation and analysis.

"Dinner's ready!" Mom called. Saved by the bell. David hopped off me and we all made our way into the dining room. Uncle Barry had laid out the dining table with the extra sections, so our comfy seating for three now fit the six of us quite nicely. He had done an amazing job, decorating with mini pumpkins and various squash and nuts. The tablecloth was a deep red and there were orange cloth napkins at every place setting. I'm surprised he didn't order an ice sculpture of a Pilgrim and a Native American embracing. Speaking of red, we hadn't said a word about my surprise visit to The Bears' Club. I had a feeling he was certain that I saw Red Walcott, but things aren't real in the South if we don't say them out loud. Besides, I couldn't even be sure why Red was there. Don't assume anything, right? And I didn't want to open that box, either. I knew better. But what I didn't know at all was how much Luke knew. Nothing at all, I imagined. If I was guessing right about Red, and Luke knew it too, would that have changed the way he felt about us being together? Stop, Derek. You cannot play the "What If?" game anymore. It's over. You've made a choice, and he's standing proudly beside you.

Mom brought the turkey in and it looked perfectly golden brown. "You'll be happy to know I did not deep fry it, David," she said, and we all laughed. "We're happy you're here with us today. You too, Bammy and Kit. Now, let's all hold hands, and Barry, why don't you start us off?"

Like every family in America, we had our own set of holiday traditions, and for Thanksgiving that meant that before we could eat we all had to join hands and say what we were thankful for this year.

"Happy Thanksgiving, everyone," said Barry. "This year, as every year, I am extremely happy for my health, first and foremost. Y'all will appreciate that when you get a bit older. I'm grateful for my loving sister, Audrey, my friends at the club, and of course, my handsome nephew Derek. I am so grateful that you came home to us this year. It has been wonderful having you back."

My mom went next. "I'll second my brother's grace and say how thankful I am for my good health. But this year is coming to a close in a most beautiful way. I have my beautiful son back, after years of him gallivanting about. I am most grateful for that. We love you so much, sweetie."

"Ya'll are gonna make me cry," said Bammy. She and Kit went next. They gave thanks for having me back in town, for their health, their families and their jobs. Kit was extra happy to be with Shawn, and I saw the look in Bammy's eyes when she said that. I hated that Bammy was alone, but I knew that love would one day come for her, too. David was up next, and I held his hand tightly.

"Well, it was a tough year for me, at the beginning," he began. "I wasn't sure how I was going to get through the spring, but I am grateful for the love and support of some amazing friends back in New York. And now? Oh, my god. Everything. Everything just came full circle, and it feels better than it ever did. Derek, I am so grateful to have you by my side again, even if I'm racking up the frequent flier miles. But I can go shopping with those points later, right? Hello, bonus! *Ha!* But, really. Thank you for giving me a second chance at this. Happy Thanksgiving."

"Wow," I said. "Every year I think I'll be able to do this without crying, but I always get a bit choked up. Mom, Uncle Barry, I am so thankful for having the two of you in my life. I have learned so much from both of you. How to be a better person, how to lead my life as an example, how to treat my friends, whom I love so dearly." I nodded at Bammy and Kit. "But most importantly, you've taught me how to love. And that's why I have an announcement to make tonight. Bammy, I love you for taking me in at the school and giving me a purpose when I came home. You have no idea how much I needed that. But now, I can feel I need something else. I'm sorry, but I need to give you my resignation. I'd like to finish the fall term, but after Christmas break, you'll need to find a replacement for me at the school. I've decided to go back to New York, for good. David, what do you think about that? David?"

I think that for the first time in a long time, David was actually speechless.

25

HOME IS A FIRE

I helped Mom clear the last of the dishes while Bammy, Kit, Barry and David rolled their bodies full of turkey and all the trimmings into the living room.

"Is that everything?" she asked.

"Yes, and it was a fantastic meal, Mom. So good. Thank you." I wrapped my arms around her and gave her a big hug. "I think we'll be eating leftovers for weeks, though. No turkey soup this year, promise?" She giggled, but I could see in her eyes that she was sad. She had something to say.

"Sweetie, I'm just a little surprised, but I understand," she said and placed her kitchen towel on the counter. "This little town couldn't hold you. I know that. We all knew that. And I can't make your decisions for you, but are you sure you are making the right choice? I know we don't talk so much about love and relationships, but if there's anything you ever want to talk about, you know I can handle it, right?"

"Mom, I love you…"

"I love you too, sweetie, but? You think I don't understand, right?"

"Mom it's just that, everything got so complicated," I said. "I came down here to clear my mind, but then everything got all twisted up with, well, with this guy, and it didn't end well."

"You mean Luke, don't you?" she said, staring me straight in the eyes.

I looked at her, dumbfounded. How did she know?

"Listen, sweetie," she said. "I know you think I'm still living in the dark sometimes, but just because I look the other way, doesn't mean I don't see or hear things. Barry and I have been friends with the Walcotts for years. Luke's a handsome man. I don't blame you. But just because he wasn't ready, should you dismiss him so quickly? I can see how you and David are together, and if you say that's what you want, then that's it. I won't interfere. But just the mention of Luke's name, and your eyes light up. And it's not just your mom who can see that."

"Mom. I don't need this. Honestly," I said, as I could feel my anger building.

"I know, honey. You hate the hard parts. You always have. You thought that coming home would be easy. That all us sweet Southerners just wouldn't understand the things you've had to deal with and we'd just rollover in your presence. But home isn't always easy, Derek. Home is a fire. All these things that we don't want to deal with on the surface just build up inside until they explode. That fire keeps growing, and you have to learn to deal with it. You've always wanted to run away when life tries to smack you down. But you can't keep running away, sweetie."

I swallowed hard as I could feel my face grow red with anger and frustration. She was right about one thing. I didn't want to face this right now. Not at all. I stormed out of the kitchen and bypassed the living room, walking out the back door to the porch. The winter sun had already set, and the air was crisp and clean. The leaves had long ago begun their transition from green to shades of yellow and red, and the back yard was a multicolored canvas lit by the floodlights.

I heard the door open behind me, but I didn't turn around. I didn't need more of my mom's faux guidance.

"Hello, Dolly," Uncle Barry said as he closed the door gently and came to stand beside me. "Your mom's a little upset in there. I don't like to see Audrey so sad, you know."

"Don't you start, too," I said, with more than a hint of nastiness in my voice. "I don't need all this 'Team Luke' shit right now, okay? How the hell did she know? Did you tell her? And he didn't want me anyway, remember? Whatever. I've already made up my mind. I'm going back to New York. I want New York."

"Funny," he said, quietly. "You want New York. That I understand. But you didn't say you wanted David."

I turned to face him, the anger building inside of me. "Fuck you, Barry. Fuck you!" I spit the words like nails. "Just because you couldn't have Red Walcott doesn't mean that I'm supposed to chase after Luke so you can live your life vicariously through me!" It was mean and spiteful, and I was ashamed of my words even as they were leaving my mouth. I could see in his face that I had hurt him, and I felt awful.

He stared straight at me and pursed his lips, slightly downward, his lower lip quivering.

"Oh, Derek. You don't know half of what you're talking about," he said. "Yes. Red was my 'boy who got away,' but that was a lifetime ago. People experiment and try things when they are young and sometimes it's just not for them. We tried. I liked it, he didn't. Sometimes you are supposed to have experiences that don't end how you want them to. That's what makes us who we are. Red and I have been friends, good friends, for years. And good friends support each other. I was there for him when Posy passed, and I'll be there for him whenever he needs me. You barged in and assumed all kinds of things, didn't you? Well, you were wrong. You want to know why Red was there? He was worried sick about his boy. His lovesick boy. That's right. Luke got up the courage and came out to him, and Red panicked. He didn't expect it, and he didn't handle the situation well. And no, I didn't tell him that you were the mystery man in Luke's life. He was there to ask me how to talk to his son, to explain to him that nothing mattered but love. That he's okay with whomever Luke loves. You can spout your politics left and right, Derek, but the truth is, some of us down here aren't as backward as you think!"

Luke came out to his dad? Luke was "lovesick?" Oh, my god. I felt everything inside of me get crushed and forced back up through my entire body. Every emotion and thought and moment of the past few months was being replayed in my mind.

I threw my hands to my face and the tears started pouring as I slowly sank to the ground.

"Oh, Dolly," said Barry, reaching down to place his hand on my shoulder and pat my back. "This will all make sense soon. It will all get figured out. Just trust yourself. You have to trust yourself."

How could I trust myself, when I didn't know what I wanted anymore? There were no clear answers, no clear path, and I was just on autopilot. I was just trying to survive, rather than live. Mom was right. Everything that I came home for, my friends, my family, the slower pace in life that I so craved, the man of my dreams who appeared as a gift, it was all burning up in front of me, daring me to reach my hand in and rescue the important things before it all just disappeared in the flames.

26

THE CHRISTMAS ASSEMBLY

"Bammy, you are running around like a chicken with your head cut off. Calm down or you're going to explode." I handed her a coffee. "Here. More caffeine."

"My lifesaver," she said. "What am I gonna do without you?"

"Drink less coffee?" I said. She laughed. It was the last day of school before Christmas break and we were in the auditorium getting prepared for the annual Christmas Assembly. The big scandal this year was a motion brought in front of the School Board by a more liberal segment of the community to change the name to the "Holiday Assembly," in deference to the "non-denominational needs of a more tolerant society." Yeah, right. That motion failed by a unanimous vote. The students had a half-day of classes, then lunch, and then they would file into the auditorium. The agenda included a few announcements, some awards and back patting, and a few songs that my theatre kids were working on. After that, they were free until the first week in January.

"I'm just so ready for this year to be over," said Bammy. "Principal Bellman is doing less and less these days. I swear, if I didn't know any better, I'd say he was out partying a few nights a week. He's come in more than a few times looking a little worse for wear. One morning he had lipstick all over his collar! And he's a married man. I think he's getting a little forgetful, if you catch my drift. I wasn't hired to be the Principal, but it sure feels like I've been acting like one all year. I just wish the pay was better."

"You're doing a great job," I assured her. Bammy had no clue that Mr. Bellman was moonlighting as "Belle" at The Bears' Club. But that wasn't my secret to tell. "They'd be foolish to not give you the job when he retires."

"Well, no matter what happens," she said, "it's just gonna suck without you here. There, I said it. I don't want to pretend anymore, Derek. It's gonna suck."

"It's always harder to be the one left behind," I said. "Trust me. I know that one well."

"Let's just get through this day and go get drunk, okay?" she asked. "Promise?"

"I promise. But right now, I have to go check on my students real quick. Then I'm running David to the airport during lunch. I'll be back right before the Christmas Assembly. Stay strong!"

I gave her a kiss on the cheek and ran down the hall. My students were locked in the choir room, rehearsing Christmas carols with the music teacher, Mrs. Powell. I opened the door to the final strains of "All I Want For Christmas Is You." That was my request. What can I say? I'm a sucker for *Love Actually*.

"Bravo!" I clapped. "Y'all are awesome! You're gonna blow them away today. Listen, I just want to tell all y'all, I'm so proud of everything you have accomplished this year. You've made me so proud to be your teacher."

"Good to know," Mrs. Powell said, drily. "Now get out of here. We're workin' on somethin'." She smiled and winked at me, and I knew that was my cue to leave.

I stepped out into the parking lot and walked towards Willie Nelson. Turning around and taking in the sight of the school for one of the last times, I realized that I would really miss this place. It's amazing how our lives can take circular routes sometimes. Life is made up of this collection of experiences, and all we can hope for is that we learn something along the way.

"Hey, buddy. Got a moment?" That voice.

"Luke…" I stammered. "Actually, no. I'm stressed for time. I need to run home and take David to the airport. He's catching a flight back to New York this afternoon."

"This'll only take a minute," he said shyly, his hands in his pockets, kicking softly at the dirt beneath his feet.

"Luke, I… listen. You were pretty clear to me at your house. I don't think it matters, anymore."

"Yes, it does matter," he said. "I need to say something. I need to tell you something."

I stopped. Could I deny him? Would anything he had to say change my mind? Are you going to let everything burn, Derek, or reach into that fire?

"Okay," I said, cautiously. "I'm listening."

He looked scared, and his whole face went white. "I have a confession," he said. "Remember when you first started working at the school, and I didn't remember you very well, and it pissed you off? Well... I did, of course. Remember you. I was lying to you, and I kept lying to you, and to myself."

"Luke, we've already..."

"No, please. Let me finish," he said. "Yes. I remembered you. But I didn't want to admit to myself that I had, because that meant I had noticed you back in high school. You stuck out. I knew you were gay, but I think that scared me, and like I said, I'm not proud of some of the things I did and said to you back then. But honestly, I realize now that I was interested in you. I just didn't understand it then. But I do now."

Of course I had hoped for this already, but I was never certain. In a way I felt vindicated. But did it change anything?

"Luke, this doesn't..." I wanted to bury my face in my hands and cry, but I had to be strong.

"Please, Derek. One more thing." He took a deep breath. "I told you before that you made me feel free. When we were... together, I felt free. Like I could do anything and be anyone I wanted to be. But I was afraid, Derek. You knew that. You saw that in my eyes. That time we spent together changed my life. *You* changed my life. You opened my eyes to a whole world of possibilities that I didn't think were available to me. After we... broke up... I, I've never hurt like that in my entire life. I had no idea I could hurt that much. I spent weeks just doing what I had to do, just to get through the day. I'm sorry I ignored you so much at school. I just couldn't face you. And then, David was here. David came back into your life, and it just crushed me. I could feel myself breaking apart. A few more weeks passed, and I woke up in bed one morning, alone, like always. I didn't want to be alone, anymore. I had to talk to someone. I told you, my parents weren't always around when I was a kid. I had Rosa. So... I talked to Rosa. I told her about us, Derek, and she opened her arms to me and I cried like a baby. But I did it. She convinced me to talk to my father, and I did. It was hard, but it was the right thing to do. He didn't take it so well, but I think he'll come around. I haven't told Lana yet, but I will, one day. Right now, though, I just feel this great weight lifted off my shoulders. I owe that to you. I do."

I could feel my knees start to get week and my face fell, betraying all the turmoil inside of me. I didn't know how to respond.

"Luke, I... I have to go," I mumbled. "David. His plane." It felt cold, but I was protecting myself. I turned to face the car.

"It was me," he said to my back, as I began to unlock the door. "In Bottom's Up. I was supposed to meet you that night. 'Cowboy' in the orange baseball cap. That was me. But when I pulled into the parking lot, I saw your car, and I lost my courage." He inhaled deeply. "I'm glad, though. That wasn't how it was supposed to happen for us. I found that courage later, at the lake. I'm glad I did. I don't regret that at all."

I pulled the door handle and climbed inside. I couldn't look at him as I drove away. My heart was aching. My uncle told me to trust myself, but right now I didn't know whom I could trust at all. The answers were getting clearer, but they frightened me.

I pulled into Mom's driveway. There were no cars there, so she and Barry weren't home. My mind was racing, but all I needed to do now was get David on that plane, and then everything would fall into place, as it should. We were on a path, and if we didn't finish, all the rules would change, again. I couldn't handle that.

As I opened the car door and walked towards the house, I heard David's voice from the back porch. Who was he on the phone with?

"*Ugh.* Tell me about it. It's been torture," I heard him say. I stayed safely around the corner. Something told me it would be best if he didn't notice me listening.

"Yes! Exactly! Like some hick backwater town in a bad 80s movie. I feel like I'm in Mayberry. It's awful. They fry everything. I half expect them to fry the water. And they're all raging alcoholics, like it's the only way they can deal with it because they know how miserable it is here. I know. *I know!* Kill me now, right? I mean, I can't spend another day here. His mom puts the smother in mother. She dotes all over him like he's this precious baby. Like she's so proud of him. I mean, yeah, he's fun and all, but he's not a superhero, you know? He's a failed actor, remember? It's his job to make you feel like you're interesting. And his uncle! That queen! You would die. Let me tell you, Nathan Lane in a dress! HA! Oh, my god. And one of his friends is like this Daughters of the Confederate Revolution thingy or another, and the other one is a Wynona Ryder wannabe, but she comes across more like Punky Brewster. These insane get ups! Yes! *Yes!* It's gonna be tough," he continued, "but we have a lot of work to do when we get him back to New York. We have to wipe this small town grime off of him and remind him who he is. Like wipe his memory or something. You should see what he's wearing these days. There's actually flannel in his closet. Flannel?! Can you believe it? And it's not like it's some vintage Gaultier or Westwood. I think it's from Target, or something. AWFUL. And he doesn't know about you, yet. No, I haven't told him. I know, *I know*. I mean, what did he expect? He frickin' runs away and I'm not supposed to have any fun? God, I miss you. Oh, yeah? Really? Is *that* what you want? Tell me more." He giggled. "My god you're so dirty! I love it. Well, we'll see if we can arrange that. I have a few days before he gets back. Then we have to find a way to open his eyes. I mean, no one's monogamous anymore, right? He can't expect that. Half the city is screwing the other half. As long as we're open about it, all three of us can have some fun, right? Oh, *rico*. I really need you, as soon as I get back. He's been running a lot and his body looks really good, but it's like his sex drive just isn't the same, yet. He doesn't do me near as good as you do, Marcos."

Marcos. Your *friend* Marcos. *Our* friend Marcos… who was going to marry us in Central Park. I wanted to throw up.

"David." I stepped out around the corner and faced him on the porch. He slammed his phone down and looked at me, panic in his eyes. He was caught.

"Derek! Babe!" He smiled, as if nothing had changed. But we both knew it had. "Are we ready for the airport? Let me just grab my bags."

"You can take a taxi," I said. "That is, if you can *find* one in this hick backwater town."

He didn't say a word as I turned to leave. He knew better.

■ ■ ■

"There you are! We've been looking for you!" Bammy saw me enter the school auditorium through the side door. "Hurry up. We're starting soon!"

"Bammy," I said, "I need to talk to you." I was clearly upset, but it barely registered with her, if at all.

"Derek, I'm sorry," she said. "I just don't have time. I promise, we'll talk after. Now you have to go sit down. Seriously. Go find your seat. It's in the front row. There's a 'Reserved' sign on it for you." There were kids running around her in circles while tables and awards and props were being shifted all over the stage behind the curtain. Bammy was definitely putting on a show. Each year's Christmas Assembly always tried to top the last.

"But, Bammy, it's really important I…"

"Derek!" She practically screeched at me. I froze. "Sorry, I'm freaking out right now. I just need to get through this. Please. We'll talk after."

I walked out from the back stage area and into the auditorium, my head cloudy with emotions. I guess my latest trauma and most current "big announcement" would have to wait. There will be plenty of time after the show. I have to remember that not everything is about me. But seriously, is this normal? Does this kind of stuff happen to normal people? My ex fiancé who I decided to gamble everything on turned out to be a truly horrible person and is now my ex boyfriend again, while the straight guy that I fell hard for but dropped because he couldn't commit is now prepared to come out, and in fact, has started the process. Meanwhile, I moved from Parkville to New York, then back to Parkville, and now I was planning to head back to New York, again. But was that for me, or for David?

I saw the "Reserved for Mr. Walter" sign and walked towards my seat. Luke was sitting three seats down, and I caught his eyes as I walked towards the row. He smiled a nervous smile, and I responded in kind, hands shoved deep in my pockets. I felt sheepish. I need to talk to him. I do. I shouldn't have walked away like I did earlier. It was a brave thing that he did, coming out to his dad and Rosa. And even more amazing, he did it for himself, not for me. I was proud of him, and I shouldn't have dismissed him so quickly. Even worse, I dismissed him for David. That prick. I can't believe that conversation I overheard. And Marcos? Holy shit, I dodged a bullet. What was I thinking? Was I blind? Was it just so easy to put on that old persona, that I didn't see what was right in front of me the whole time? You can't go backwards, Derek. Learn that lesson once and for all. Like Tommy said, when it comes to relationships, I have a learning disability.

Christmas music was playing through the speakers and the house lights began to flicker off and on, signaling for everyone to take their seats. The prerecorded music was slowly silenced and the audience grew quiet, waiting for the spectacle to begin. Suddenly, from behind us, we heard the opening sounds of the marching band playing "We Need a Little Christmas," from *Mame*! The band marched down the aisles, working their way to just below the stage, as the curtains opened to reveal the cheerleading squad in pyramid formations. They had choreographed an entire routine to the song, ending with the smallest girl being thrown high into the air, then landing safely in the arms of the two strong boys on the squad. We all jumped to our feet and cheered as Bammy took the stage and walked up to the microphone.

"Now that's some Christmas Commodore spirit, isn't it?" She clapped loudly. "Can I get a 'Go, Commodores' from y'all?"

"Go, Commodores!" we all yelled back. We had school spirit, yes we did. At least, I felt it. I loved this school, my students, my life here. I even began to feel some of that Christmas spirit that had eluded me for so many years. The Christmas dance was tonight, and it was time to announce the students who had been elected to the Christmas Court. When I went to Parkville High, the Christmas Court was the exclusive realm of jocks and cheerleaders. But things had changed. Some of my theatre kids crossed over into sports. Some of the art students ranked high in the "in" crowd. One of the cheerleaders had the highest grade point average in her class and was on track to being elected Valedictorian. I was proud that our little school had become quite the diverse microcosm of society, especially here in the South. My first impressions were wrong. Things *had* changed here.

Football season was over, so Luke was up next to hand out awards. But to Bammy's credit and influence, there were also awards for science, math and the arts. Seeing the looks on the students' faces as they were rewarded for their efforts really filled my heart. We were doing good work here, and I was proud to be a part of it. The choir was up next to finish the show, and then we could be on our way. Mrs. Powell came out to the stage, her back to the audience. I could see her reminding the students to smile as they sang "All I Want for Christmas Is You." I looked over at Luke and he was smiling broadly at me. Blatantly. Did I miss something? Bammy had pulled so much together; I half expected to see Hugh Grant appear on stage at the end of the number.

But, no. Bammy had something else up her sleeve.

"Thank you, Mrs. Powell." She started her closing remarks. "Weren't they wonderful? Just wonderful." We all clapped our approval. Why were the students remaining on stage?

"I'd like to thank all of you for coming today," she continued, "but before we go, we have a little something extra special for you. As many of you know, Mr. Walter won't be returning after Christmas break. He's leaving us for New York City." The audience started to boo their disapprovals. They were booing! I felt humbled, and sank in my seat a bit.

Bammy, stop, please. What are you doing? This is why we needed to talk.

"We have been so blessed to have him here this semester, and I know he will be missed by many of us." She looked pointedly at me, then at Luke. My heart skipped a beat. This was too much. I didn't ask for this. "So, the students asked if they could put together something for you Derek, and with the help of Mrs. Powell, here it is. Derek, this is for you. Take it away, kids!"

The opening synthesizer chords started as four dancers from the Pompon Squad took the stage with members of the Flag Corps standing to the sides. It was choreographed to perfection, and when the voices started singing, I could feel my heart lifting and a grin take over my face.

I couldn't believe it. They picked Madonna. "Lucky Star." For me! I wanted to cry happy tears, but I knew I had to get through it. They finished strong, and I was on my feet in no time, along with everyone else in the audience. The applause was thunderous, and when it slowed down, suddenly the cries of "Speech! Speech!" began.

I held my hands up to quiet them, as I turned to face the audience from my front row seat. "Thank you! Thank you so much. I'm really, really overwhelmed," I said. "So overwhelmed, in fact, that I'm going to make this easy. Here's the thing. I have an announcement to make. I was thinking about this on my way here, but y'all have convinced me. I've decided... not to leave." A huge cheer erupted, and suddenly the throngs of kids rushed forward, grabbing me from every angle. "That is, of course, if Vice Principal Talbot will still have me?" I yelled over the crowd. I turned to look at Bammy, and she was grinning wildly, two thumbs up. Students surrounded me, high fives and hugs all around. I could see Luke walking over to me, and when he held his hand out to shake my hand, I grasped it. What he did next though, I did not expect.

He pulled me into his arms and held me tightly.

"Can we start over again? Let's start fresh," he whispered in my ear.

"Hi," I said, into his. "I'm Derek."

"I'm Luke," he said, and he continued to hold me, not caring who was watching. And that was all I needed to know that I had made the right decision, finally.

27

WHAT ARE YOU DOING NEW YEAR'S EVE?

It was snowing outside and The Firelight was filled to maximum capacity. We could have opted for something fancy for New Year's Eve, but instead we opted for comfortable. Kit was here with Shawn, Tommy had Meredith by his side, and even Bammy had a date.

"Michael," she said as she introduced him all around, "this is Kit and Shawn, Tommy and Meredith, and this is Derek and his boyfriend, Luke. Derek and Luke and I work together, remember?"

"How could I forget?" he said. "So nice to meet y'all. Bammy talks about you non-stop. She's pretty impressed with you two," and he looked pointedly at Luke and me.

"Well," I said, "she's pretty special to us. You could say she helped us find each other, in a way."

Luke was standing behind me, his arms around my waist. "It's almost time, babe. I'm going to go grab two more bottles of champagne."

"Sure thing," I said, as I turned to kiss him. He smiled and headed towards the bar. Bammy and Kit were all over me in no time.

"Well, don't the two of you look cozy?" Kit remarked. "He sure has made a lot of progress in a few weeks."

"It's like a floodgate," I said, sipping champagne. "Once you open those doors, you can't really turn back."

"His slutty stage is next, right?" asked Tommy, lifting his glass to drink.

"How the hell do you know that?!" asked Meredith.

"Oh, Tommy and I have been friends forever," I said, all of us laughing. "Trust me. You don't have anything to worry about with him. He's just heard all my stories."

"Well," said Bammy, "whatever stage is next, at least he'll be with you."

"Yeah," I smiled. "He is. With me." It just felt funny to say it. But it was true. After the Christmas Assembly, Luke and I spent the whole night in his apartment, talking over everything that had happened. He had his reasons, his regrets, and I had mine. We both made mistakes, but the important thing was that we found each other in the end. Like Barry had said, we had to trust ourselves, and it all worked out.

"Speak of the handsome devil," said Bammy, as Luke walked over with two new bottles of champagne. The bartender followed with a round of shots. We topped up our glasses with champagne, and then passed around the shots of whiskey.

"I'd like to make a toast," said Luke. "To Derek. Thank you for opening my eyes to possibilities I didn't even know existed. You made my year, and I can't wait to see how next year unfolds, with you at my side. Bottom's up, Duke!" And he winked at me, our own private joke. This man! I just had to smile.

"Duke!" Kit exclaimed. "Derek and Luke. *Duke!* Oh, my god. *I. Love. That!*"

The bartender stood on the bar and yelled. "Get ready, y'all!" We all turned to watch the big screen television, as we saw the mirrored light ball beginning its slow descent from the top of One Times Square. New Year's Eve was always the coldest night of the year in New York City, and I shivered a bit as I stared at the huge crowds gathered outside in Times Square.

"You miss it, babe?" Luke asked, one arm tight around my waist.

"Not at all," I said. "I have everything I need right here."

I was home.

ACKNOWLEDGEMENTS

I am grateful for and humbled by the assistance I received along the way from many wonderful friends who donated their time and efforts into helping me create the work you are reading, my first novel. I could not have done this without you.

Thank you Karyn Adams, Bridget Benn Chapman, Zan Crowder, Gina Pope Moore, Marcos Pagan, Brian Semple, Jesse Summers, Cynthia Tady, Bethany Wright Tillman and Angie Vicars for your tireless eyes, your helpful corrections and your meaningful suggestions.

Thank you Nicolás Chifflet and Patrik Nerséus for the amazing book cover and website, and Mauri Chifflet and Emil Klang for the fantastic promotional video.

Thank you to my parents, Linda, George and Mary. You always encouraged me to be true to myself, and for that I am eternally grateful.

And finally, to my own Scooby Gang, spread out across the globe. You are all amazing, beautiful, people, and I am truly blessed to count you as my friends.

Remember, you are what you take time to become!

ABOUT THE AUTHOR

Jordan Nasser was conceived in California, born in Washington, raised in Tennessee, schooled in France, lost in the South, found in New York City, and is currently thriving in Stockholm, Sweden. He knows what it feels like to be far from home—and how to make a home for himself in new places.

A graduate of the University of Tennessee, he worked as the Global Head of Digital for the international fashion retailer H&M. Then, much like his character Derek, Jordan decided to take a risk and change his life, so he left the workplace to write a book.

Home Is a Fire is his first novel, and he is extremely grateful for your support.

www.jordannasser.com